NEVER FORGET LOVE...

"I love you!" Nerissa whispered.

"That is what I wanted you to say," the Duke said. "And I love you." Then he was kissing her...demandingly, passionately. Only when they were both breathless and Nerissa with a little murmur hid her face against the Duke's shoulder did she say in a voice that was curiously unsteady:

"But my sister...Delphine. She must...never know!"

"She will have to know one day," the Duke said, "for I intend that you will be my wife, Nerissa. In fact, I cannot live without you!"

"You will...have to!" Nerissa cried. "How could I face Delphine when she is absolutely sure you will ask her to marry you? I love you desperately...but I can never marry you!"

The Duke put his fingers under Nerissa's chin to tilt her small face up to his. Then he was kissing her and the rapture and wonder of it carried them once again towards the stairs...

A CAMFIELD NOVEL OF LOVE
BY BARBARA CARTLAND

A NEW CAMFIELD NOVEL OF LOVE BY

BARBARA CARTLAND

Never Forget Love

A JOVE BOOK

NEVER FORGET LOVE

A Jove Book/published by arrangement with
the author

PRINTING HISTORY
Jove edition/January 1986

ISBN: 0-515-08442-5

Jove books are published by The Berkley Publishing Group,
200 Madison Avenue, New York, N.Y. 10016.
The words "A JOVE BOOK" and the "J" with sunburst
are trademarks belonging to Jove Publications, Inc.

PRINTED IN THE UNITED STATES OF AMERICA

AUTHOR'S NOTE

WHEN I wrote this book, the house I was talking about as "Lyn" is really Longleat, the most beautiful ancestral home in England.

Longleat, which belongs to the Marquess of Bath and is the most perfect example of Italianate Elizabethan architecture in the country.

It began as a Priory built by the Augustinian Canons and was sold for 53 pounds to Sir John Thynne in 1515 when Henry VIII dissolved the Monasteries.

It is so beautiful and ethereal that one expects it to float away into the sunshine.

The Great Hall with its stone-flagged floor and hammer-beam ceiling support is unchanged since 1559. In the Red Library there is a copy of Henry VIII's Great Bible of 1641.

Queen Elizabeth I was entertained in the State Dining Room in 1574, and of course there is a ghost.

I have not written about the Longleat ghost, but one which came to me in a dream, and which I find rather fascinating.

Never Forget Love

chapter one
1818

"YOU are late!" Nerissa said as her brother came in through the front door and threw his riding-whip down on a chair.

"I know," he answered, "but you must forgive me. I was riding an animal which at least had spirit in him, and I was making the most of it!"

Nerissa smiled.

She knew that to obtain a horse of any sort to ride was a delight that Harry prized above everything else.

Sometimes, when she was struggling with the house-work, or the stove in the kitchen which was so old that it was always going wrong, and a dozen other problems were cropping up every day, she would imagine that one of her father's books suddenly became a success and overnight he was famous and they were rich.

It was such an impossible dream that she laughed at herself for being so childish, and yet she longed above everything else for Harry to have the horses he wanted and the clothes that would make him as smart and fashionable as his friends at Oxford.

No one could be more handsome, she thought, though he was wearing a threadbare old riding-coat that he had worn for years, and that she had mended and darned until she thought there was little of the original material left.

It was not surprising, because their father even though he was now grey-haired and his face was lined, was still an extremely good-looking man.

In fact, Nerissa sometimes wondered to herself why after her mother had died some woman had not tried to capture her father.

Then she laughed again at her fancies because it was doubtful if Marcus Stanley was aware there was a woman in the world when he was concentrating on his books which examined and recorded the development of Architecture in Britain.

Harry had admitted quite openly that he was not clever enough himself to understand his father's work, and although Nerissa loved him she did at times find his long descriptions somewhat dull.

They were however acclaimed by the Architectural Society, although the sales amounted to such an infinitesimal number of volumes that the income derived from them was almost non-existent.

Nevertheless she was proud as she dusted the shelf in the Library, to see the row of five large volumes all bearing her father's name.

Harry was pulling off his riding-boots which were covered with mud and Nerissa said:

"I hope you thanked Farmer Jackson for giving you one of his horses to ride."

"He thanked me!" Harry replied. "He said that having bought the horse, he was almost afraid to get on its back

2

and had been looking forward to my coming home. He knew that if anyone could break the animal in, it would be me!"

Nerissa looked at the dirt not only on his boots but also on his breeches, and her brother knew what she was thinking.

"All right! He threw me twice! The second time I had a bit of a job to catch him, but by the time I took him back to the Farm he was beginning to realise I was his master."

There was a relish in Harry's voice which Nerissa did not miss, and she said:

"Come into the Dining Room as soon as you have washed your hands, and I will tell Papa that luncheon is ready, as incidentally it has been for over an hour!"

"I do not suppose Papa will have noticed!" Harry remarked, and Nerissa knew this was true.

She went into the kitchen where there was a savoury smell of stewed rabbit and an old woman with rheumaticky hands was taking the hot plates somewhat unsteadily out of the oven.

"Let me do that, Mrs. Cosnet," Nerissa said quickly, knowing how many things had been broken by her in the past.

She saved the plates at what she thought was the last moment, and carried them into the Dining Room before running back to lift the stew off the stove and pour it into a china dish.

Having set it down on the dining room table, she ran across the small hall to the Study, where her father was working.

"Luncheon is ready, Papa," she said, "and hurry, because Harry is back and he is hungry."

"Is it luncheontime?" her father asked vaguely.

Nerissa resisted the temptation to retort that luncheon was long overdue and if Harry was hungry, so was she.

Reluctantly leaving the manuscript he was writing and the book he was using for reference on top of his desk, Marcus Stanley rose and followed his daughter into the Dining Room.

"You have done a good morning's work, Papa," Nerissa said as she put some of the rabbit stew onto his plate, well aware as she did so that it was overcooked. "You must take a short walk after luncheon before you go back to work. You know it is bad for you not to get some air."

"I have just reached a most interesting part of my chapter on the Elizabethan period," her father replied, "and of course it is easy for me to quote this house and to describe how the bricks, although they have mellowed with the ages, have defied the weather as well as the years, and are in far better shape than bricks made two hundred years later!"

Nerissa did not answer because at that moment Harry came into the room.

"Sorry to be late, Papa," he said, "but I have had a splendid ride on a horse that was as wild as a coot until I began to make him see sense!"

Marcus Stanley's eyes rested on his son's smiling face reflectively as he said:

"I remember when I was your age finding an unbroken horse an irresistible challenge."

"I am sure you would enjoy it now," Harry said.

As he spoke he took the plate his sister was handing him and started to eat ravenously.

Watching him, Nerissa wondered a little wistfully if she could manage during the University vacation to have sufficient food in the house to keep Harry satisfied.

4

It was difficult enough when he was away to stretch the very meagre amount of housekeeping money, which was all her father could allow her, to supply them with their needs.

But with Harry "eating them out of house and home," as she expressed it to herself, it was impossible not to run into debt, or worse still, to fear that her brother, although he never complained, was hungry.

Rabbit was their staple standby at all times of the year, but she was thinking the farmers would soon be shooting the pigeons that destroyed the young crops, and Harry had often said he enjoyed the way she roasted them.

She could not help thinking wistfully that baby lamb was in season, but it was a very long time since they had tasted one.

What she could usually afford was an old sheep later on, which would be knocked down in price because it would be very tough unless very carefully cooked.

It was a blessing, she thought, as she put a mouthful of rabbit to her lips that her mother had been an exceptionally good cook, and had shown how to make the dishes her father and Harry enjoyed, and also how to make a meal seem larger than it really was.

Potatoes, of course, were invaluable, and roasted, fried, boiled, or sautéed, they filled up the gap when a helping of meat, because it was so expensive, could not be very large.

"Is there any more, Nerissa?" Harry broke in on her thoughts.

"Yes, of course," she replied.

She gave him everything that was still in the dish except for a spoonful which she added to her father's plate, knowing he was far away in Elizabethan times, and therefore eating automatically and, she suspected, without the slightest idea of what he was actually putting into his mouth.

There was a new cottage loaf on the table, and Harry cut himself a large slice to finish up the gravy.

"That was good!" he said with relish. "No one can cook rabbit like you, Nerissa! The rabbit they serve up at Oxford is quite inedible!"

His sister smiled at the compliment, and collecting the plates and the empty dish she carried them into the kitchen.

She had been wise enough to make a filling pudding, knowing how much exercise Harry was taking, and the sponge had risen light and golden.

All she had to do now was to pour it over the home-made strawberry jam which she had preserved last year, and which with the minute amount of cream she had managed to skim off the top of the milk would make, as far as Harry was concerned, a satisfying dish.

To finish the meal there was only a small piece of cheese left. Nerissa intended to go shopping this afternoon, but Harry had eaten far more than she expected at yesterday's luncheon, which had been very much the same as he had today.

Having finished his portion of pudding, her father rose from the table.

"Will you excuse me, Nerissa," he said, "if I go back to my work?"

"No, Papa!" Nerissa said firmly. "You know you ought to take a little exercise first, so I suggest you walk to the end of the orchard and see how those new fruit trees we put in are coming along. We had to do something, if you remember, after we lost some of our most precious trees in the March gales."

"Yes, of course," her father agreed.

Then, as if he thought by hurrying he would get an unwelcome task over quickly, he went out into the hall, picked up his old felt hat that was almost in tatters, and went out through the garden door into the sunshine.

Harry laughed.

"You bully him, you know!"

"But it is so bad for him to be cooped up in that stuffy Study all day and all night!"

"It may be bad for his health, but it makes him happy."

There was a pause before Nerissa said:

"I am not so certain about that. I often feel that he misses Mama so intensely that the only way he can forget her even for a short while is to concentrate almost fanatically on what he is writing."

Her voice was very soft and gentle as she spoke, and Harry, looking at her, said perceptively:

"You miss Mama too!"

"Terribly!" Nerissa answered. "Nothing is the same without her. When you are away and Papa seems at times not even to know I exist, I feel as if I cannot bear it!"

"I am sorry," Harry said sympathetically. "I had no idea you felt like that, and I suppose it is very selfish of me to have all the fun of being at Oxford while you slave away here."

"I do not mind 'slaving' as you call it," Nerissa said. "It is just that sometimes I never see a soul from one day to the next, except of course when I go down to the village. They are very kind, but it is not the same as being with Mama or having her friends coming to see her."

"No, of course not," Harry agreed. "What has happened to them?"

"They were kind in their way after Mama died, but

they wanted to talk to her, not to a girl of seventeen as I was then, and even when they were generous enough to ask me to a party of sorts I usually had no way of getting there, and worse still, nothing to wear."

Harry was silent for a moment. Then he said:

"I have only another year at Oxford, and after that I will be able to earn some money and we shall all be in a better position. I suppose it would not be a sensible idea for me to leave before I get my Degree?"

Nerissa gave a little cry.

"No, of course not! It is absolutely essential that you should stay your full time. A Degree is very important! Of course it is!"

"I realise that," Harry said, "and I have worked really hard this term. My Tutor is very pleased with me."

Nerissa walked round the table to put her arms round her brother's neck and kiss him.

"I am very, very proud of you," she said. "You are not to take any notice of me if I grumble. I am so lucky to have you home, and of course to have Papa—when he remembers that I exist! It is very ungrateful of me to 'whine like old Mrs. Withers.'"

This was a local joke, and Harry duly laughed.

Then he put his arms round his sister's waist and said:

"I am going to try to think up some special treat for you, so you had better make yourself a new gown."

"A new gown!" Nerissa exclaimed. "How do you think I can pay for one?"

"'Where there is a will there is a way!'" Harry replied lightly. "That is what Nanny always said, and perhaps the best thing we can do is to have a day of fasting and the money we save will go to decking you out like the Queen of Sheba!"

"That is certainly an idea!" Nerissa laughed. "I can

see exactly the sort of gown I should get after such a gruesome sacrifice!"

"I tell you what I suggest..." Harry began.

What he was going to say was forgotten because there came a loud and unexpected rat-tat on the front door.

Brother and sister looked at each other.

"Who can that be?" Harry asked. "Whoever it is, they sound very impatient. Are you expecting the Duns, or the Bailiff to confront you with an unpaid bill?"

"No, of course not!" Nerissa replied.

She took off the apron she had worn while she was preparing and clearing the luncheon and walked from the Dining Room across the hall to the front door.

Harry did not move but picked up a large crumb which had been left on the table and put it into his mouth.

Then he heard his sister give an exclamation that was almost a cry of astonishment.

As he rose to his feet he heard Nerissa say:

"It cannot be! But it is! Delphine!"

"I thought you would be surprised to see me!" a sophisticated voice answered, and Harry walked from the Dining Room into the hall to stare in astonishment at the woman who had just arrived.

She was dressed in the peak of fashion with a high-crowned bonnet trimmed with small ostrich feathers, the colour of which matched her gown, which was covered with a cape trimmed with fur.

She walked two steps farther into the house and looking round said:

"I had forgotten how small this was!"

"We thought you had forgotten us!" Harry said bluntly. "How are you, Delphine, or is that an unnecessary question?"

Then the Vision stopped still to stare at him, taking

in with shrewd eyes his height, his looks, and his untidily tied cravat.

"How you have grown, Harry!" she exclaimed.

"It is not surprising when you have not seen me for six years!" Harry replied. "And I must say, you look very 'up to scratch'!"

"Thank you," Delphine said with just a touch of sarcasm in her voice.

Then she said in a different tone that was almost brusque:

"I want to talk to you both, and I suppose there is somewhere where we can go to sit down?"

"Come into the Drawing Room," Nerissa said. "It is unchanged and I am sure you will remember it."

She opened a door at the far end of the hall and went into a low-ceilinged room which her mother had always used on special occasions.

In it was all their best furniture and all the most precious things they possessed, and the most attractive of the Stanley ancestors hung on its panelled walls.

Delphine walked in, her silk petticoats beneath her gown swishing with an expensive sound as she did so.

Then taking off her cloak with its expensive fur edging, she handed it to Nerissa before she seated herself in an armchair at the side of the fireplace.

She was however not looking at her sister, but at the room.

"This is just as I remember it," she said, "and of course it looks its best in the evening in candlelight."

"We do not often sit here since Mama died," Nerissa said. "Instead we use Papa's Study, or the Morning Room, when Harry is at home."

As she spoke she did not think her sister was listening and she wondered why Delphine was here and how she could suddenly appear without giving them any warning.

Four years older than Harry and five years older than Nerissa, Delphine had, when she was eighteen, married Lord Bramwell who had seen her by chance at a garden party given by the Lord Lieutenant of the County and had lost his heart.

He was a very much older man and Delphine's mother had been doubtful if she was wise in accepting his proposal of marriage.

"It is something you should think about very carefully, dearest," she had said, "because, after all, you have not met many men and Lord Bramwell is so very much older than you are."

"He is rich and important, Mama, and I want to marry him!" Delphine had replied obstinately.

She had not listened to her mother's pleas for her to take her time in considering whether it was a wise move, nor would she agree to a long engagement.

Because there was no other valid reason why Mr. and Mrs. Stanley should not agree to their daughter marrying Lord Bramwell, Delphine had her own way in everything and was married with what seemed almost precipitate haste.

And when she had driven away in his smart carriage drawn by four well-bred and well-matched horses, she had passed out of their lives.

Looking back, Nerissa could hardly believe it had happened.

One moment Delphine had been one of the family, happy, Nerissa had believed with their father and mother, her sister and Harry, in their ancient Elizabethan house known as Queen's Rest.

The next minute she had vanished completely and, as far as they were concerned, she might never have existed.

She had been in Paris when Mrs. Stanley had died four years later, and she had not returned home for the Funeral.

She had written her father a short, rather cold letter of condolence, and that was the end.

To Nerissa, who had loved her sister simply because she was one of the family, it had seemed completely incredible.

Even the excuse that Lord Bramwell lived in London and had a country house in a County far distant from theirs did not comfort her in losing one of themselves.

"I wrote to her for her birthday," Nerissa said once to Harry, "but she never replied."

"Delphine has no further use for us," Harry said. "She is very smart and is acclaimed as one of the Beauties of St. James's."

"How do you know that?" Nerissa asked.

"My friends at Oxford have talked about her and her name is always in the Social Columns. Last week they said she was the most beautiful woman at Devonshire House, which is known for having more Beauties per square inch than anywhere else in the country!"

Harry had laughed and Nerissa knew that it amused him.

But for her, it was not only incredible, but she felt deeply hurt that her sister no longer cared for her or even for their father.

Now looking at Delphine she could at least understand how she had been acclaimed as the most beautiful woman in London.

Delphine was very lovely. Her hair was the gold of ripening corn, her eyes a vivid blue, her complexion flawless.

She was the same type as Georgiana, Duchess of

Devonshire, and the other lovely women who Nerissa heard about from Harry, and who were lauded by the young men who followed the Prince Regent's lead.

Delphine was thinner than she remembered her and she had developed, Nerissa thought, a kind of seductive, sinuous movement with her hands, and her long neck had something very sensitive about it.

Now, as Harry also seated himself, there was a little pause before Delphine said:

"I thought you would be surprised to see me, but I have come back because I want your help."

"*Our* help?" Harry ejaculated. "I can hardly imagine how we can help you! I have heard about your husband's horses and I know he won the Two Thousand Guineas two years ago!"

There was a little pause before Delphine said:

"My husband is dead!"

"Dead?"

Nerissa sat bolt upright in astonishment.

"Do you mean to say, Delphine, you are a widow? But why has no one told us?"

"I suppose you cannot afford the newspapers!" Delphine said scathingly. "Actually he died twelve months ago, and I am now out of mourning, as you can see."

"I am sorry!" Nerissa said softly. "Do you miss him very much?"

"Not in the slightest!" Delphine said coolly. "That is why I need your help."

"He cannot have left you penniless? Oh, Delphine, how can we help you?"

"No, of course not!" Delphine snapped. "I would hardly come here asking you for money. As a matter of fact, I am extremely well off. It is something quite different from that."

"Then what can it be?" Harry asked. "Incidentally, Delphine, you have hurt Nerissa and Papa very much by not communicating with us all this time."

Delphine made a graceful movement with her hands.

"It was difficult," she said. "My husband was not interested in my family, and why should he be?"

"So you were glad to get rid of us," Harry said bluntly.

"It was not exactly like that," Delphine answered. "I had set out on a new life, and I wanted to forget the miseries of the past."

"Miseries?" Nerissa questioned.

"All that pinching and saving, never having decent clothes, and never really enough to eat," Delphine said.

Nerissa drew in her breath, but she said nothing and her sister went on:

"But we are still of the same blood, and I cannot believe you will not do for me what I want."

"Tell us first what is it," Harry said.

The way he spoke made Nerissa certain he was thinking, despite what Delphine had said, that she must be wanting money in some way and the only possible economy they could make would be for him to leave Oxford.

Instinctively, without being aware of it, Nerissa put out her hand towards Harry as Delphine said:

"It may surprise you, but I am going to marry the Duke of Lynchester!"

It was now Harry's turn to be astonished and he sat up in his chair and exclaimed:

"Lynchester? I do not believe it!"

"That is not very complimentary," Delphine said. "I thought you would be very proud if I were the wife of the Premier Duke of Great Britain, the most important of all the Peerage!"

14

"If you want the truth," Harry said, "I think it would be a miracle. When are you to be married?"

There was a perceptible pause before Delphine replied:

"To be truthful, he has not asked me as yet, but I know he intends to do so."

"Then if you will take my advice," Harry said, "you will not 'count your chickens before they are hatched'! I have heard a great deal about Lynchester. Who has not? Although his horses gallop past the winning-post to carry off every trophy, no woman has yet managed to gallop him up the aisle!"

"But that is what I intend to do," Delphine said in a hard voice.

As if she felt Harry was questioning her ability to do so, she looked at him somewhat aggressively, and brother's and sister's eyes met across the room defiantly.

Then Nerissa said:

"If the Duke will make you happy, dearest, then of course we will give you all our good wishes, and I am sure when you tell Papa about your engagement he will in fact, be very proud."

"He will also be very interested," Harry interposed, "because Lynchester has the finest Elizabethan house in the country, and that is the period on which Papa is working at the moment."

"If that is so," Delphine said quickly, "then it could be a great help."

"Help for what?" Nerissa asked.

Her sister was silent. Then she said:

"Now try to understand what I am going to tell you. The Duke of Lynchester has been pursuing me for the last two months, and I am almost certain it is only a question of days before he asks me to be his wife."

She made a little sound that was almost a cry of triumph and went on:

"Think what that will mean! Next to the Royal Family, I shall be one of the most important people in the country. I shall be the chatelaine of a dozen houses, the most magnificent being Lyn in Kent. I shall be able to wear jewellery that will make every woman I meet green with envy, and I shall go down in history as being the most beautiful of all the Duchesses of Lynchester!"

The way she spoke made Delphine's voice sound as if it were accompanied by a fanfare of trumpets.

Then Nerissa said very quietly:

"Do you love him very much?"

"Love him?" Delphine asked. There was a pause before she went on: "But he is a difficult man—one never knows for certain what he is thinking—besides being cynical with all those women falling at his feet and pleading with him just as much as to notice their very existence."

She gave a little laugh that was not a particularly pretty sound as she added:

"But he *has* noticed me! He has singled me out and made me the talk of London, and now we are both guests at a house party given by the Marquess of Sare."

Harry raised his eyebrows.

"So you are at Sare Castle!" he exclaimed. "That is only five miles away!"

"Yes," Delphine answered. "That is why I was able to come here, since all the men have gone out riding."

"I bet they will have some jolly fine horses!" Harry said beneath his breath.

"Now, what the Duke has said," Delphine went on, "is that he would like to see my home, and he has therefore suggested that he and I should dine here tomorrow evening!"

As she finished speaking there was complete silence, and she was aware that her listeners were staring at her in such astonishment, it seemed as if their eyes might pop out of their heads.

"Dine here?" Nerissa ejaculated. "But how can you possibly . . . do that?"

"The Duke has arranged that we arrive for dinner at seven o'clock. I have told him about Queen's Rest, my ancient home, where Queen Elizabeth rested on one of her journeys, and of course about Papa's preoccupation with architecture. Surprisingly the Duke had actually heard that Papa wrote books on the subject."

"But . . . how can he possibly dine . . . here?" Nerissa asked desperately. "What can I . . . give him to . . . eat?"

"That is what I am going to tell you," Delphine said, "and why I have come to see you."

She glanced round the Drawing Room as if to reassure herself. Then she said:

"This room looks all right if you arrange more fresh flowers and of course make sure the candles are all new. The same applies to the Dining Room. I expect it is just as shabby as it always was, but at least the pictures of our ancestors are impressive, and the furniture is all in keeping with the house."

"But . . . Delphine . . . !" Nerissa began.

"Now, listen," Delphine interrupted. "The Duke has no idea that either of you exist, and I see no point in suddenly producing a family that he might think would be an encumbrance on him."

"Where can we go if we are not here?" Harry asked sharply. "And you are not going to have much to eat unless you bring your food with you."

"I have thought it all out," Delphine said slowly, "and although Nerissa will be here, the Duke will not see her."

"Then where shall I be?" Nerissa asked.

"In the kitchen!" Delphine replied. "Which is where either you or Mama have always been!"

"Are you . . . saying that I am to . . . cook your dinner without being . . . introduced to the man you . . . intend to marry?"

"That is putting it quite simply and sensibly," Delphine answered.

"And . . . who is supposed to . . . serve the meal if I am . . . not to come into the Dining Room?" Nerissa enquired.

There was only a moment's pause before Delphine's eyes turned towards Harry.

There was no need for her to speak.

"I am damned if I will do it!" Harry said. "You walk out on us, Delphine! You did not answer the letters Nerissa wrote to you, you did not even come back for Mama's Funeral! You have all our good wishes that you get your Duke, and I hope he makes you happy, but we are not helping you to get your claws into him in a dirty, underhand manner which, quite frankly, is not cricket."

Delphine was not perturbed by the way her brother spoke. She only said:

"I cannot believe that you would be so foolish as to refuse to help me when you hear how I shall express my gratitude for such services."

"I personally, and I think I speak for Nerissa, have no wish to hear any more," Harry said, "and I am certain if Papa knew what you are suggesting, he would be horrified. We may be poor, Delphine, but our blood is as good as, if not better than, anything that runs in the Duke's veins! And we have something which perhaps

18

has been omitted from his makeup, which is called 'pride!'"

To her brother's surprise Delphine laughed.

"That sounds a very characteristic Stanley speech!" she said. "It should be added to the stories Papa and Mama used to tell us when we were children of how brave the Stanleys were in battle, how they supported King Charles II while he was in exile, how they patted themselves on the back because they were so well-born and it did not worry them if their pockets were empty. That is all very praiseworthy, but personally I prefer money."

"As you have made very obvious!" Harry said sarcastically.

"I should have thought you would find it useful too," Delphine said. "What I was going to suggest, before you interrupted me so rudely, is that if Nerissa and you will do what I wish, then I am prepared to pay you the sum of three hundred pounds."

She paused, and it seemed as if neither Harry nor Nerissa could breathe.

Then Nerissa murmured almost beneath her breath:

"D-did you . . . say three hundred pounds?"

"It is a sum of money which would supply Harry with the sort of horse he was always bellyaching to have," Delphine replied. "I was sick to death of his complaints. It would also make certain, my dear sister, that for once you had a decent gown rather than what you are wearing at the moment, which would shame a Gypsy!"

Delphine spoke scathingly, but Harry was repeating as if he could not believe it to be true:

"Three hundred pounds!"

"You can have it now," Delphine said, "but of course Papa must know nothing about it. He still believes money is unimportant in comparison with some old bricks and tumbledown buildings which interest nobody but himself. But surely, you two, because you are young, have a little more sense?"

"How can you afford to give us so much money?" Nerissa asked.

"I can afford it," Delphine replied, "because I am gambling on making my background as a Stanley look good enough for the Duke to realise he will not be lowering himself in asking me to be his wife."

"But . . . if he loves you . . ." Nerissa began, "surely your ancestry is not all that important?"

"I am only grateful that none of my friends can hear you talking such nonsense!" Delphine said rudely. "You cannot imagine that the Duke of Lynchester, who can have any woman he likes in the whole Kingdom, is going to make a *mésalliance* when it comes to marriage! I could be his mistress, I am well aware of that, but I am determined — yes — determined to be his wife."

She spoke with a resolution in her voice which made Nerissa remember how as a child she had often defied her mother in one way or another and always eventually got her own way.

"If you ask me," Harry said, "I think it is an insult that the Duke, or any other man, should look you over as if you were a horse and decide whether you have enough good points for him to wish to own you!"

"That is a vulgar way of putting it, Harry, but it is the basic truth," Delphine said. "You cannot be so stupid and unsophisticated, as Nerissa is, not to know that in the Social World in which I move one's antecedents and one's blood are of paramount importance when it comes to marriage. A Doxy is one thing, a Duchess is another!"

Harry laughed.

"I will say one thing about you, Delphine you are very plainspoken!"

"I am fighting for something that matters to me very much," Delphine said. "Now, let me ask you to answer yes or no—are you or are you not going to help me?"

Feeling as if it was too big a question for her to answer, Nerissa looked at her brother.

Three hundred pounds seemed to be dancing in front of her eyes, telling her what a difference it could make to them all, and especially to Harry.

She knew as she looked at him that a battle was going on within him.

While he instinctively disliked any form of deception and untruth, he was tempted as she was by the idea of so much money, especially when it meant he could buy a horse.

It could also provide him with some clothes, and he remembered that before he went back to Oxford he was going to beg Nerissa to find enough money to provide him with a new evening suit.

The one he was wearing at the moment was in rags, and one of his fellow students had told him that next term they might be asked to a dinner at Blenheim Palace.

Slowly he said, as if he were thinking of the words as they came to his lips:

"If we refuse to help you, Delphine, what will you do?"

"If you refuse and I lose the Duke, I will hate you and curse you until the end of my life!" Delphine replied. "He has asked to see my Elizabethan home which I described to him in such glowing terms, and to meet my very distinguished father. Surely there is nothing wrong in that?"

"What is wrong, as you well know," Harry said quickly,

"is turning your sister into a cook, and me into a butler! But I suppose we can pretend we are playing Charades, and hope to God the Duke never suspects he is being deceived!"

Delphine gave a cry of horror.

"If he does, it will be because you are two incompetent fools!" she said. "But if we succeed, I shall be the Duchess of Lynchester!"

There was a look in Delphine's eyes which told Nerissa she had won a victory she had never intended to lose.

But as she looked at her sister she had a strange, unaccountable feeling that Delphine would never wear the Duchess's strawberry-leaf coronet.

chapter two

"DELPHINE has certainly thought of everything," Nerissa said as she walked to the kitchen table.

"Where it concerns herself," Harry replied.

His voice was not really sarcastic, as he was too excited over what was happening.

Already he had seen a horse which he thought might suit him, although as he said to Nerissa, he knew he must be cautious as the 150 pounds which was his share had to last a very long time.

It was Harry who had insisted that Delphine give it to them before she left.

"Perhaps I would be wise to see that you first carry out my instructions properly," she said.

Harry had laughed.

"If you think we are trusting you to do that, you are making a mistake!"

Delphine stared at him angrily, and he had continued:

"You still owe me a pair of riding-boots that you promised me before you married Bramwell if I would help at the Wedding Reception, as you wanted me to."

Delphine looked slightly shamefaced.

"I admit I forgot," she said after a moment as if she had no desire to annoy Harry.

"Well, that shows how much your promises are worth," Harry teased. "So Nerissa and I would much prefer to be paid in advance."

Nerissa made a little sound of dissent, feeling it was very embarrassing to hear Harry talking to her sister in such a way.

Then as if she half-appreciated his distrust, Delphine had laughed and drew an envelope from her bag.

To Nerissa's astonishment, it contained the money, in notes, she had promised them, and she said quickly before anyone else could speak:

"We must put it in a safe place, and then in a Bank as quickly as possible."

"That is sensible of you," Delphine approved, "for if you lose it or it is stolen, I am certainly not paying out a second time."

Harry had taken the money from her and said:

"Thank you, Delphine, I can assure you every penny of this will be put to very good use."

"As long as you carry out what I have asked you to do, Harry, I am not complaining," Delphine said sharply. "But I shall be extremely angry if you make a mess of it."

There was a note in her voice which told Nerissa how important the dinner was to her, and how much she wanted to impress the Duke with her distinguished home.

But it was not very pleasant to know that neither she

24

nor Harry were thought good enough to meet their sister's future husband.

After Delphine had gone Harry said:

"'It is an ill wind that blows nobody any good!' Just think what we can do with all this money!"

"I wish we could have refused it," Nerissa said in a low voice.

To her surprise Harry agreed:

"That is just what I felt like doing! It would have given me the greatest pleasure to tell Delphine that we would not accept payment for helping her, but would do so simply because we are the same flesh and blood."

He spoke sharply and Nerissa knew that his pride was hurt.

Then he said lightly:

"I am prepared to dress up as a Hotentot or pretend I am a baboon if it means I can buy a decent horse and some clothes in which, for a change, I am not ashamed to be seen."

Because he sounded like a small boy receiving a Christmas present, Nerissa did not express her own feelings but she knew that she felt Delphine was degrading not only the two of them but the whole family.

"Once she is a Duchess we shall never see her again," she told herself, remembering how Delphine had behaved after marrying Lord Bramwell.

There was, however, so much to do that she had no time to think, but only to get down to work.

Delphine had not been exaggerating when she said she had brought everything they would require for the dinner, for when Nerissa saw the amount of food that was piled on the kitchen table she could hardly believe her eyes.

There was a leg of baby lamb such as she had longed to buy for her father, a salmon which she knew had been caught fresh from the river that flowed only a few miles from the Marquess of Sare's house.

Somehow in some clever way of her own, Delphine had persuaded the Marquess's Chef to put in everything that was required for the cooking: fresh pats of butter, a huge pot of thick cream, herbs, and young vegetables fresh from the garden.

There was also fruit which Nerissa guessed must have come from the Marquess's hothouses.

There were all the ingredients for soup with which to start the meal, and small fresh mushrooms for the savoury to end it.

Nerissa could not help being amused when she knew that although when she had been at home Delphine had never expressed any appreciation of the delectable dishes that her mother had cooked for them, she had obviously noted how they were done and at this moment was putting her memory to good use.

When Harry had gone off blithely to look at every available horse in the neighbourhood, she had worked methodically to get everything ready for the evening meal.

She had laid the table in the Dining Room, putting fresh candles in the rooms as Delphine had suggested, and found time to pick all the flowers that were coming into bloom in the garden, and arrange them in bowls in the Drawing Room, the hall, and the Dining Room.

'If I had time,' she thought, 'I would like to polish all the furniture, but I doubt if His Grace would notice it.'

She had asked Harry to tell her more about the Duke of Lynchester, and to her surprise he knew quite a lot.

"He is not only admired," he said, "because he is a

Duke. You should hear my friends at Oxford talking about him—but also because he is the most notable sportsman in the whole of England."

He thought Nerissa looked at him slightly quizzically and he said:

"It is true, he has the finest horses anybody could afford, but he is also a magnificent rider himself, a Corinthian, and a pugilist, besides being, as I was told last term, a champion fencer."

Harry spoke in an awed voice and was surprised when Nerissa laughed.

"I do not believe it!" she said. "There must be a snag somewhere!"

Harry grinned.

"Of course there is, but it is something I should not be telling you."

"Tell me," Nerissa pleaded.

"If you want the truth, he is a devil with the women," Harry replied, "and in my own mind I very much doubt if he will marry Delphine."

"But she is so certain that he will!"

"A lot of other women have been certain before her," Harry said. "The sister of one of my friends, who was a widow after Waterloo, threatened to kill herself if the Duke would not marry her."

"Kill herself?" Nerissa cried.

"Apparently he led her to believe he really loved her, then inevitably became bored, and went off after somebody else."

"He sounds horrible and cruel!" Nerissa exclaimed.

"I have no reason to stick up for him," Harry said, "but actually that is rather unfair. If women pursue a man, they should not whine and complain if he eludes them and lets them down."

Nerissa looked at her brother as if she did not understand. Then she asked:

"What do you suggest they do?"

"Let him chase them!" Harry replied. "The man should be the hunter, not the hunted!"

He spoke in a way which made Nerissa's eyes twinkle.

"Is that what you are?"

"Of course!" he said. "But I have to admit that without a penny to my name, no woman with sense would chase me, except for my handsome face!"

"That is the most conceited remark I have heard!" Nerissa exclaimed, and threw a cushion at him.

Harry threw it back, then they were laughing and for a moment the Duke was forgotten.

When about an hour and a half before dinner Harry had come downstairs carrying some clothes over his arm, Nerissa had said curiously:

"What have you got there?"

"I thought as Delphine was determined to make us into servants," he replied, "I might as well do it properly. I remembered we had some of our grandfather's old livery up in the attics, and I found a coat which fits me, although it is rather tight, a pair of white knee-breeches, and one of the striped waistcoats with crested buttons on it."

"I had forgotten they were there!" Nerissa exclaimed. "If you can get into them, you will certainly look the part."

"I left my own evening clothes at Oxford. You know I always wear an old velvet coat here to be comfortable. But I do not expect that Delphine would be very impressed with that on the family Butler!"

Nerissa looked at Harry reproachfully.

"I am sure she would have been horrified if you had

appeared looking harum-scarum, but nevertheless far more like a gentleman than a servant."

"Now I will be able to make my sister proud," Harry laughed, and held up a white wig that his grandfather's footman had worn.

Having cleaned the silver buttons, he went upstairs to put on the clothes while Nerissa thought she should remind her father once again what to expect.

He had been surprised when she told him Delphine had called and was bringing the Duke of Lynchester over the following evening especially to meet him.

"Lynchester!" her father had exclaimed. "Well, it will certainly be interesting to talk to him about his house. It is exactly what I want for my chapter on Elizabethan architecture. I believe there is no house in the country so well-preserved as Lyn."

"We are going to make a special effort to please the Duke, so do not be surprised at what you have to eat, Papa, or that we have someone waiting at table."

"Waiting?" her father murmured. "Who will that be?"

"Farmer Jackson's oldest son, George," Nerissa said quickly. "Apparently he is quite proficient at it, so you need not worry that he will make mistakes."

She had chosen Farmer Jackson's son because he was tall like Harry, and she thought her father, who was always incredibly vague about such things, would never suspect for a moment that the temporary butler was really his own son.

A short while later when Harry came into the kitchen wearing the family livery and his hair covered with the wig, she thought for one moment that he looked ridiculous.

Then she knew the clothes were exactly what a servant

29

in a big house would have worn as a gentleman's footman or outrider.

"As you said—we are doing Delphine proud!" she remarked.

Then she laughed as Harry assumed a broad country accent saying:

"Good day, t'Yer Grace, an' Oi 'opes as 'ow Yer Grace'll enjoy th' evening wi' us country bumpkins!"

"Oh, Harry, do not make me laugh!" she pleaded. "At the same time, if you do anything like that, Delphine will be furious, and I am sure she will ask for her money back."

"I would like to 'pull her leg,'" Harry said, "but as you wisely point out, it is not worth risking those lovely golden guineas that are going to buy me a horse with which I am determined to win the next Point-to-Point which Sare has on his estate."

"If you do enter for it, you will have to be careful not to let him realise who you are," Nerissa warned. "He might tell the Duke, and as far as he is concerned, you and I do not exist."

"I will remember that," Harry said, "but I cannot think why Delphine is not honest enough to admit that she has a brother and sister."

As he spoke he looked at Nerissa and anybody watching him would have realised there was suddenly a dawning look in his eyes.

The two sisters were very much alike, but for the first time Harry saw that Nerissa, who as the youngest of the family had always seemed a child, had grown into a lovely young woman.

He did not say anything, but he told himself that it was only right that Delphine should pay for her decep-

tion, which was both insulting to them and as regards
the Duke positively feline.

*   *   *

The Duke's carriage drew up outside the front door at
exactly ten minutes to seven and Harry already had the
door open and had rolled a very old piece of red carpet
over the steps.

He gasped with admiration when he saw the horses
come to a standstill.

He knew each one would have cost far more than
Delphine had given Nerissa and him in payment for their
services.

He could not help wishing that just for once in his
life he might have the opportunity of driving such thor-
oughbreds, or better still, riding them.

But he remembered his role and waited at the open
doorway as a footman resplendent in the Duke's livery
got down from the box on the carriage to open the door.

The Duke stepped out first and at a first glance Harry
knew that all the things that he had heard said about him
by his friends were true.

Never had he imagined that any man could look so
tall, so broad-shouldered, so elegantly and fastidiously
dressed and at the same time be so obviously athletically
masculine.

'That is what I want to look like,' Harry thought.

Then as his sister stepped elegantly from the carriage
in rustling silk and with a whiff of exotic perfume passed
by him into the hall, he managed to bow his head sub-
serviently and take the Duke's top hat from him and help
him off with his evening cape.

Delphine did not wait for Harry to announce them, but moved eagerly, like a young girl, across the hall and through the open door of the Drawing Room.

"We are here, Papa!" she cried, forcing what seemed to be a spontaneous lilt into her voice.

Nerissa, on Delphine's instructions, had already arranged that her father would be waiting for them at the end of the Drawing Room.

However old his evening clothes might be, Marcus Stanley looked extremely distinguished and very much a gentleman.

Delphine kissed him lightly on the cheek, saying as she did so:

"It is wonderful to see you again, Papa, and looking so well. May I introduce the Duke of Lynchester, who has brought me here."

"I am delighted to see you," Marcus Stanley said, holding out his hand, "and I have in fact all the afternoon been reading about Lyn and your ancestor who originally built it."

The Duke's rather severe expression lightened in a smile as he replied:

"I know which book you mean, Mr. Stanley, and I feel it must have been very heavy going."

"On the contrary, I found it absorbingly interesting, and giving exactly the information I require for my own book at the particular point I have just reached. So meeting you now could not be more opportune."

"Before you start on your favourite subject, Papa," Delphine interposed, "I want you to pour us a glass of champagne. I am well aware that once you start on Early English architecture, no one will speak to me for the rest of the evening."

She looked at the Duke as she spoke and he replied:

"You know that is untrue. However, to make you happy, I promise, however interesting your father may be, I will still remember you are present."

"I hope I can compete with the glories of Elizabethan England," Delphine said, "but I am rather afraid that I will be overlooked."

"I think you are fishing for compliments," the Duke replied.

At the same time his eyes rested on her appreciatively, as Delphine was very much aware.

She had taken a great deal of trouble with her appearance that evening, knowing it would be a mistake to look too flamboyant or make the Duke suspect that she was in any way "showing off."

Instead, she wore a gown of periwinkle blue that accentuated the blue of her eyes, and which coming from Bond Street had been extremely expensive, but managed to look deceptively simple.

She also wore round her long neck a necklace of turquoises and diamonds, and there were turquoises in her ears as well as round her wrists.

They were very much less ornate than most of her jewels, on which the Duke had already complimented her.

She glanced round the Drawing Room, noticing with relief that the candlelight concealed the threadbare carpet and faded curtains.

"It is lovely to be home," she said in a soft, girlish voice, "and when a house means as much as this house means to me, it does not matter whether it was built three hundred years ago or yesterday. What is important is that it has always been a place of love."

The Duke did not answer, but Delphine was sure that his hard eyes softened and she thought his glance lingered for a moment on her lips as if he longed to kiss them.

By the time Harry announced in a slightly gruff voice, so that his father should not recognise it, that dinner was served, Delphine told herself with satisfaction that the evening was going well.

Although her father was talking somewhat ponderously of his book and the exhaustive research he had made in the Elizabethan period, the Duke was only too willing to speak of his own house and the labour and care that had been expended there to produce one of the finest examples of architecture in Elizabeth's reign.

"It seems extraordinary to us now," the Duke was saying as they sat down at the Dining Room table, "that the materials came from so many places at the cost of what must have been an enormous effort in those days."

"I have always heard how exceptional Lyn is," Marcus Stanley was saying as they sat down.

"I can honestly say there is not a house to equal it in the whole length and breadth of the land," the Duke said boastfully. "My father said once he had never found a woman who could keep him entranced, captivated, and enthralled as Lyn managed to do. When I am there I sometimes feel like saying the same thing."

Delphine gave a little exclamation of horror, and the reproach in her eyes was very moving.

"Is that what you still think?" she asked.

"Shall I say there are exceptions to every rule?" the Duke replied.

The smile she gave him in response was radiant.

Dinner was superlative, and Harry fetching the last course from the kitchen said:

"His Grace has praised every dish so far and left nothing on his plate, so you have certainly fulfilled your part of the contract!"

"Has Papa any idea who you are?" Nerissa asked.

"He never gave me a second glance," Harry replied. "He is centuries away, supervising the building of Lyn, and if he had looked, he would very likely have thought I was a ghost."

Nerissa laughed, and handing him the savouries said:

"Take them in quickly before they get cold, and after that there is only the coffee."

"Thank goodness!" Harry exclaimed.

Nerissa got coffee ready in the silver coffeepot she had cleaned earlier in the day, and poured some of the cream which Delphine had brought into the prettily fashioned silver cream jug that matched it.

When Harry finally came back from the Dining Room he sat down on one of the kitchen chairs and said:

"Thank goodness that is over!"

"You remembered to leave the decanter of port in front of Papa?"

"I remembered everything!" Harry answered, taking off his wig and throwing it down on the table. "And now, if you will forgive me, I am going to take off this coat which is far too tight under the arms and makes me feel as if I were in a straitjacket."

"It certainly made you look the part," Nerissa smiled. "I am sure that even Delphine will not be able to complain."

"Certainly not," Harry said. "She has made her point, the Duke has been duly impressed with her ancient home and her distinguished father, and I doubt if we will see her again until this husband dies and she is chasing another!"

"Oh, Harry, you should not say such things," Nerissa protested. "The Duke is a young man and poor old Lord Bramwell was very old!"

"I suppose, if you think about it," Harry said, "when Delphine has caught her Duke she cannot expect to go much higher, unless she catches sight of an eligible Prince or a King!"

The way her brother spoke sounded so funny that Nerissa laughed, and rising from the table she said:

"Now I am going to give you your dinner—and you deserve it! There is some delicious salmon to start with, then the baby lamb, which is what I have always longed to be able to afford."

"I can assure you I shall do justice to both," Harry said.

Nerissa moved towards the stove, and as she did so there was the sound of men's voices coming along the passage outside.

For a moment she thought she must be mistaken, and yet they came nearer and she could hear her father talking and wondered what could have occurred.

She knew that Delphine would have left the gentlemen to their port and gone upstairs, as she had told Nerissa she would do, to tidy herself.

"Do not forget to light the candles in your bedroom," she had said sharply. "I do not want to go there in the dark."

"No, of course not," Nerissa said. "I had thought of that."

If Delphine was upstairs, why was her father coming towards the kitchen?

They drew nearer and now, just when Nerissa was certain he would pass on down the passage, the kitchen door opened and he came in, followed by the Duke.

For a moment she and Harry were too surprised to do anything but appear to have been turned into stone as her father walked into the middle of the kitchen to say:

"Now, as you see, Your Grace, this is a perfect example of an Elizabethan ceiling which has never been touched except for very minor repairs over the centuries. Look at those joists and the strength of the ships' timbers which have kept it in such good condition for so long."

Only as the Duke did not answer did Marcus Stanley realise that his younger daughter was staring at him in consternation, and his son, for some unknown reason in his shirt-sleeves, was sitting at the kitchen table.

If Nerissa and Harry were surprised, no less was the Duke.

He had expected, when his host wished to show him the unique architecture of his kitchen, he would find there the usual old family servants that would somehow have been in keeping with the atmosphere of the house.

Instead, he saw facing him a young girl whose looks struck him as vaguely familiar.

Her hair was very fair, the colour of the sun when it first rises over the horizon, her eyes that seemed to dominate her whole face were green flecked with gold, and the translucence of her skin seemed to shine like a pearl against the ancient walls by which she was surrounded.

He was also aware that she was staring at him, not only with surprise but also with consternation that seemed to him to have a touch of fear about it.

Then to break the sudden silence there was the sound of quick footsteps outside in the passage, and a moment later Delphine came into the kitchen.

One glance at her face told her sister how angry she was, and after an awkward pause, during which nobody spoke, Nerissa managed to find her voice.

"I am ... sure ... Delphine dearest," she said, "you

37

are . . . surprised to see us here . . . but Harry and I . . . came back unexpectedly to find the . . . poor old Cosnets had been . . . taken ill and rather than . . . spoil your dinner party . . . we took their place."

The words came from Nerissa's lips a little disjointedly, and as she spoke she saw some of the anger leave her sister's face and again there was a silence, as if Delphine were trying to assimilate what had been said.

Then she managed to answer:

"This is a surprise! You told me both you and Harry would be away!"

"I . . . know," Nerissa said, "but the . . . children in the house where we were . . . staying developed . . . measles and as we were in the way, we . . . came . . . back."

Listening, Harry wanted to applaud, knowing that Nerissa's brain had worked quicker than his had been able to do.

He rose belatedly to his feet as the Duke said:

"I find this somewhat bewildering, and I would like to be introduced if this young lady was really responsible for the superb meal I have just enjoyed."

As if Marcus Stanley was suddenly aware of what was happening, he said:

"Yes—yes, of course! This is my younger daughter, Your Grace. Nerissa. And this is my son, Harry, who has just come down from Oxford."

Nerissa curtsied and the Duke held out his hand, saying:

"I really must congratulate you, and may I say in all honesty that I have never enjoyed a better dinner."

Nerissa smiled.

At the same time she was conscious of the firm grip of his hand, and as she looked into his eyes she had the feeling, although she thought she must be mistaken, that he was not being deceived.

Before she could really formulate what she was feeling, the Duke was shaking hands with Harry.

"I am sure you are enjoying Oxford," he said. "What College are you at?"

"Magdalen, Your Grace."

"Where I was myself," the Duke said. "I do not expect it has changed very much."

"The College is very proud of Your Grace."

"I hope that is true," the Duke replied, and Nerissa thought the way he spoke made it obvious he would be very surprised if it was not.

Delphine came a little farther into the kitchen, and as if she thought she must take part in the Play that was taking place in front of her eyes, she said:

"I suppose, Nerissa, I should thank you for 'saving the ship,' so to speak. I would have been very upset if the Duke and I had had to drive away supperless!"

"As it is, I have been feasted and fêted," the Duke remarked.

"And now I think we ought to go," Delphine said.

Nerissa knew as she spoke that she was longing to get away, longing to repair the damage that had been done by her father's unforeseen behaviour.

"I might have guessed," Nerissa chided herself, "that Papa would want to show anyone who was interested in Elizabethan architecture the ceiling of the kitchen. He has always said it is the one absolutely unique piece of building in the whole house."

"Before I leave," the Duke said, raising his head to the ceiling, "I must look carefully at what you are showing me, Mr. Stanley. I do agree that no later century has produced such fine workmanship or anything so serviceable that would last as long as this has, for nearly three hundred years."

"I thought you would appreciate it," Marcus Stanley said with satisfaction.

Behind his back Delphine gave Nerissa a meaningful glance, and she understood it was not only what had happened which had infuriated her, but also her own appearance.

Quickly, thinking she should have thought of it before, she removed the apron that she had worn to cook the dinner, realising as she did so that the gown she was wearing beneath it was not very much more presentable.

However, as if they were still very conscious that things had gone wrong, Harry was shoving himself back into his liveried coat, and now as the Duke brought his eyes down from the roof he would have been very obtuse if he had not realised that three people in the kitchen were willing him to leave as quickly as possible.

"This has been a unique experience for me," the Duke said, "and, Mr. Stanley, I would feel it very wrong if I did not return your most agreeable and instructive hospitality."

He paused, which made what he was saying more impressive.

"I want to suggest that in return, you, your two daughters, and your son should do me the honour of being my guests at Lyn next Friday. A Horse Show is taking place in the grounds on the Saturday, but if you could all manage to stay until Tuesday, that will leave two days in which I can show you my Elizabethan masterpiece, as you have shown me yours."

For a moment, as her father did not reply, Nerissa held her breath.

Then with a smile Marcus Stanley said:

"It will not only give me great pleasure to see Lyn, Your Grace, but it will be of inestimable benefit to me as an author to be able to view with my own eyes what at the moment I am able to describe only from hearsay."

"Then that is agreed," the Duke said. "I will send a carriage here for you, your son and daughter early on Friday morning—shall we say nine o'clock? I will arrange for you to have luncheon on the way and you should arrive, if my horses perform as they should, at Lyn at about teatime. Of course, your elder daughter will drive down with me from London."

The Duke looked at Delphine as he spoke, and with an effort she forced a small smile to her lips before she said:

"I would love to come to Lyn, but I expect it will be impossible for Nerissa and Harry to accept your invitation. After all, they are both very busy here."

"I hope you can manage to set aside your numerous engagements," the Duke said politely, but Nerissa knew he did not believe a word of it.

As he spoke Nerissa looked uncomfortably at Delphine who was making it very clear that she was not to accept. But Harry had other ideas.

"If you are having your Horse Show on Saturday, Your Grace," he said, "I cannot imagine anything more exciting! I have heard of the Horse Shows that take place at Lyn, and one of my friends who was there last year said it was the finest parade of horses one is likely to see in the whole of the British Isles."

"I believe that is its reputation," the Duke agreed, "and I expect you would also like to see my stables. So do not forget to pack your riding-clothes."

"I will certainly do that," Harry said.

There was a note of excitement in his voice which would have told the most obtuse listener that he had just been offered a ticket to Heaven.

"Then that is agreed," the Duke said, "and since I have no intention of allowing any of you to refuse, please be ready for the carriage on Friday morning, and I shall be waiting to welcome you at the end of your journey."

As he finished speaking the Duke walked from the kitchen and there was nothing Delphine could do but follow him and her father.

However as she reached the door she paused for a moment and looked back to say with her beautiful face contorted with fury:

"Why did you not stop the old fool from bringing the Duke in here?"

Her words seemed to be hissed from between her lips.

Then as Nerissa made a helpless gesture with her hands she flounced out of the kitchen, leaving a charged atmosphere behind her.

"Phew!" Harry exclaimed.

Then before he could say anything more Nerissa said:

"Quick! You must go to see them off and do not upset Papa by letting him think he has ruined the evening. I know how thrilled he is at having been invited to Lyn."

Harry did not reply, but merely ran from the kitchen and down the flagged passage, and only as his footsteps died away did Nerissa realise she was trembling.

It had been such a shock when the Duke had walked into the kitchen and an even bigger one when Delphine had followed him and shown how angry she was.

However there had been nothing she or Harry could do about it, and it had never crossed her mind that her father would want to show the Duke the kitchen ceiling.

He was of course proud of it because it was, as she knew, unique.

At the same time, who would have expected the owner of Lyn to be interested in the kitchen of some obscure Manor that he had never heard of until he met Delphine?

She could only pray that she had managed to cover up the truth by pretending that she and Harry had taken the place of servants who were actually nonexistent.

When Harry came back a few minutes later, he said as he sat down again at the kitchen table where his salmon was waiting for him:

"It was extremely quick of you, Nerissa, to save the side. At least I hope we did! I thought, in fact, the Duke looked slightly more cynical than usual."

"You do not think he . . . believed me?"

"I should be surprised if he did!"

"Why should you say that?" Nerissa asked.

"Because he is known as being very shrewd, and if he did not see through Delphine's wiles, then he is not as clever as I have always believed him to be!"

There was a pause before Nerissa asked.

"Were they . . . very obvious at dinner?"

"She did everything but kiss his boots!" Harry said. "If that is the way all women behave towards Lynchester, then all I can say is I am not surprised he prefers being a bachelor!"

Nerissa gave a little cry.

"Oh, Harry, do not say that! It might be unlucky! If he does not propose to Delphine now, she will say it is our fault and will never forgive us."

"I cannot think it will make much difference," Harry said. "We have not seen her for years, and if she marries Lynchester, I should be very surprised if we ever saw her again."

He took a mouthful of salmon before he said:

"That is why I intend to see the Horse Show and ride the Duke's horses while I have the chance. Once she is married to him, mark my words, Delphine will say we are dead, diseased, crippled, or transported—anything to prevent our visiting the august presence!"

"But why, Harry? Why should she be like that?" Nerissa asked him. "We were all so happy together when we were young and Mama was alive."

"I can answer that question quite simply," Harry replied.

"Then what is it?" Nerissa asked in astonishment.

"Look in the mirror, old girl!"

Nerissa laughed.

"Now you are talking nonsense! You are not going to tell me that Delphine is jealous of me?"

"Why not? You are very lovely—exactly like Mama! If you ask me, now that I have seen you together, Delphine is an obviously older, considerably overpainted edition of you!"

"Harry! How can you say such things?" Nerissa asked.

Because it made her feel apprehensive for Delphine, she hoped that what Harry had said was untrue.

chapter three

As she drove away with the Duke from Queen's Rest, Delphine thought with a sense of fury that her father had messed up what had been in her opinion a perfect plan.

It had never entered her mind for one second that when she left the men alone in the Dining Room her father might take the Duke to visit the kitchen.

Because she had always been extremely bored with architecture, even that of her own home, she had never listened to what her father was saying either to the family or to guests.

Now, however, she remembered too late that anyone who was interested in architecture was always taken to see the kitchen ceiling.

At the same time she knew the one thing she must not do was to let the Duke think she was upset.

When she first realised, to her intense satisfaction, that the Duke of Lynchester was turning his roving eye in her direction, she had decided with a determination that would have made strong men quake that he would marry her.

She had heard about the Duke long before she first saw him, and when she had done so she understood how it was impossible for any woman not to admire him and find him irresistible.

It was not only his title and his distinguished position in the Social World, it was that he himself was, without exception, the most attractive man she had ever seen.

The stories of his love affairs lost nothing in the telling.

Practically every woman she met was only too willing to relate her own particular story about the Duke, which was either his latest *affaire de coeur* or one of those which had ended so disastrously in tears, threats of suicide, and broken hearts.

Although Delphine was still young in years when she became a widow, she had grown immeasurably older during the time she had been married to Lord Bramwell.

She had not been unhappy, because she found the fact that he was rich enough to give her almost anything she wanted was fascinating after being so poor and insignificant.

That her husband was so much older than herself did not particularly trouble her either.

That she found him a bore went without saying, but as he was infatuated with her she soon learned how to make the very best of his feelings.

She found that she could soon turn every kiss he gave her into jewels or gold.

When Lord Bramwell died, leaving her, to all intents and purposes, a rich woman, she told herself that now was her opportunity to rise up the social ladder to the highest possible pinnacle.

When she saw the Duke of Lynchester she knew exactly what her goal was.

Delphine was far too shrewd not to know that in order to capture the Duke, where so many other women had failed, she had to be different.

This meant quite simply that she refused the moment he began pursuing her to go to bed with him.

Every other woman, she learned, who had been in the same position had found him so overwhelmingly irresistible that they had succumbed at the first assault and ardently given him everything he desired.

The reason for this was that the women with whom the Duke spent his time were either widows like herself or had, as was fashionable, extremely complaisant husbands.

Occasionally, Delphine had learned, a husband would be brave enough to challenge the Duke to a duel, but invariably and unjustly, he became the loser of the contest.

He would then have to face the laughter of his friends when he appeared with his arm in a sling, while the Duke, undoubtedly the villain of the piece, got off scot-free.

"Why do you refuse me, Delphine?" the Duke asked when he realised to his surprise that she was adamant in saying no.

"I have been brought up very strictly," Delphine explained in a sweet, girlish voice, "and my mother gave me ideals which I would not wish to lose."

"How would you lose your ideals by loving me?" the Duke asked. "After all, as a widow, you are beholden to no one, and also I think you told me your mother was dead."

"Yes, she is dead," Delphine said in a pathetic tone which would have made any man wish to comfort her, "and I miss her so very much!"

"What about your father?"

This was just the question Delphine was hoping for.

The Duke was well aware of his own consequence, and Delphine knew he would never take as his wife a woman who was socially beneath him or whose blood did not match his.

It was because he had inherited his title early that he had not been pressured into an arranged marriage when he was a very young man.

Now that he was thirty-four, Delphine guessed he was beginning to admit it was time he produced an heir, and was looking for the right woman with whom to share his life.

She knew he would want to respect his wife, and what he had given no woman in the past was his respect.

'That is what I must get!' she thought.

She then set out to entice, excite, beguile, and, she hoped, enslave him.

At the same time she locked her bedroom door and resisted all his pleadings, which were very voluble, that they should find happiness in each other's arms.

"You make me very happy," she told the Duke, "when we do things together, and quite frankly, Talbot, I love you."

"But not enough to make me happy," the Duke said reproachfully.

It was with difficulty that Delphine refrained from saying that he only had to offer her a small gold wedding ring and she would agree to anything he suggested.

Instead, she ran away from him, but not so fast that he could not catch up with her very easily.

She had tried almost every enticement she had ever known, including cancelling at the last moment an agreement to drive with him, which had only made him angry.

Then when he mentioned her father she decided that this was her opportunity to impress him once and for all with her suitability to be his Duchess.

He had, of course, heard of the Stanleys, since they featured in every history book.

There had been no battle since Agincourt in which they had not played some part, nor had there been a victory at sea at which a Stanley had not been honoured or acclaimed.

There were many leading Statesmen in the Stanley family tree, and it was only belatedly in her acquaintance with the Duke that Delphine realised that, if Lyn was a perfect example of Elizabethan architecture, so was Queen's Rest.

She had always in her heart of hearts despised her home because the house itself was not large enough to be impressive like the mansions and Castles in which she had stayed once she was married.

There were no footmen to wait on her father and mother, and no valuable horses in the stables to carry them wherever they wished to go.

"How could I have endured another year of such misery?" she used to ask herself once she had left home with Lord Bramwell, and had determined never to return.

Now as she extolled the past virtues and bravery of her family, she fancied there was a faint expression of disbelief in the Duke's eyes, as if he knew she was making them out to be of more importance than they really were.

She also felt perceptively that he would never propose marriage to any woman until he had seen her background and the stock from which she came.

She was turning over in her mind how she could take the Duke to meet her father at Queen's Rest, when they both received an invitation from the Marquess of Sare, who Delphine remembered lived only a few miles away from her own home.

It was infuriating for her to think that when she was a girl the Marquess and Marchioness had never included her or Harry in the invitations they sent once a year to Mr. and Mrs. Stanley, inviting them to a garden party.

It was the one concession the Marquess and his wife made to what they called "the locals," and the only occasion on which they entertained outsiders.

"Now I am very much inside!" Delphine told herself with satisfaction, and she began to plan how she could take the Duke over to meet her father and make sure at the same time that he did not encounter Harry or Nerissa.

She had long ago determined that they were of no consequence in her life and best forgotten.

Harry might be tolerated because he was a man, but the idea of having a sister and one who was obviously going to be like her mother who had been a great Beauty made Delphine shiver.

She had told all her friends in London that she was an only child.

"I was such a lonely little girl," she said to the men who wanted to talk about her childhood.

"That is one thing you will never be again, my darling," was the obvious reply.

Her head would go back against their shoulders as they kissed her demandingly and passionately until she knew it was very unlikely she would ever be lonely again.

After her husband's death Delphine had taken several lovers, and indeed one shortly before it.

She was however very discreet, and the majority of her women friends thought she was too much occupied with herself to be very interested in men.

Delphine subtly contributed to this idea and gave the impression, which she knew was talked about, that she was, in fact, cold and unresponsive to any man, however attractive.

In actual fact she was fiery, passionate, and insatiable.

She found it very difficult to refuse the Duke, and it might have become impossible if she had not been having a secret and wild affair with Lord Locke.

Lord Locke was everything Delphine admired and enjoyed in a man, and if she were capable of giving her heart to anyone, it would have been to him.

Unfortunately he was not well off, had no important ancestral home in the background, and nothing to recommend him except that he fell passionately and uncontrollably in love with Delphine.

Sometimes she would play with the idea that the world was well lost for love in the shape of Anthony Locke.

Then she knew she would never be satisfied unless she carried a strawberry-leaf coronet on her head, could sit with the Duchesses at the Opening of Parliament, and entertain at Lyn and at all the Duke's other magnificent houses.

"Why could I not have been a Duke?" Anthony Locke would ask despairingly.

To make him happy Delphine would say:

"I love you just as you are!" and then there had been no need for any other words.

Now, as the horses passed through the gates at the end of the drive which had been broken ever since Delphine could remember, she slipped her hand confidingly into the Duke's and said:

"It was sweet of you to be so kind to Papa, and I know he is thrilled at the idea of seeing Lyn."

"I think he is the only living author who writes really ably about the Elizabethan period," the Duke said reflectively.

"Papa is very clever," Delphine said with a little sigh. "I only wish I took after him."

"You do not need a brain as well as beauty," the Duke answered.

But he did not, as Delphine expected, put his arms around her, and she therefore moved a little closer to him to lay her head against his shoulder.

"I am glad you have seen my home."

"It was all extremely interesting," the Duke remarked, "especially the ceiling in the kitchen."

Delphine drew in her breath. Then when she would have changed the subject the Duke asked:

"Why did you not tell me that you had a brother and a sister? I always believed you to be an only child."

"They were so much younger than I was that they played very little part in my life."

It was the best Delphine could do, and she was well aware there was a sharpness about the Duke's voice as he asked:

"It seems very strange you should not have mentioned them. How old is your sister?"

"She is very young," Delphine replied, "about seventeen, I think, and I am afraid she will feel very out of place at one of your sophisticated house parties."

"I am sure you will be able to look after her."

Delphine, who had been intending to coax him into agreeing it was a mistake to include Nerissa in the party, knew that whatever objections she made they would be overruled because he had made up his mind.

She had already had experience of the Duke's iron will and had thought it equal to her own. Yet while she had every intention of getting her own way and marrying him, she suspected it was the last thing he was contemplating.

She however made one last effort.

"Perhaps it would be better," she said, "if you had Papa to stay at another time, when you do not have the distraction of the Horse Show."

In the darkness of the carriage she did not realise that the Duke's eyes were twinkling as he replied:

"I cannot believe that you could be so hard-hearted as to deprive your brother of what he could not conceal is the most exciting invitation he has ever had!"

"No, of course not!"

Then the Duke asked:

"I imagine you are contributing to his education at Oxford. It is quite obvious that your father is not well off."

Delphine drew in her breath sharply before she said quickly:

"Papa makes some money from the sale of his books and of course as we have land there are the rents from the farmers who lease it from us."

Because she was afraid of what the Duke would answer to this, she put up her hand to touch the side of his face and said:

"Now we have talked enough about me! Let us talk about you, dearest Talbot! There is no subject more entrancing!"

She managed with what she thought was considerable expertise to keep that subject going until they reached the Marquess's house, where there was a large party waiting to reproach them for having been away for so long.

"You missed an excellent dinner!" someone said, and the Duke replied:

"I doubt if it was as good as the one I enjoyed, and now that we are back it is up to you to entertain us."

To Delphine's anger, instead of inviting her onto the dance floor, where a small Orchestra was playing for those of the Marquess's guests who preferred to dance, the Duke sat down at a card table and she knew it would be impossible to talk with him intimately again before they retired to bed.

For the first time her resolution not to become his mistress wavered a little, and she played with the idea of going to his side and asking quietly so that nobody else could overhear, to come to say good night to her.

Then she thought that would be a very silly thing to do, but as she went up to bed she had the uncomfortable feeling that since the visit to Queen's Rest something had gone wrong, although she was not certain what it was.

"I am tired, and I am just imagining things," she told herself as she got into bed.

But she found it hard to sleep and kept seeing Nerissa's young face in front of her eyes.

Then she told herself that the Duke never had been and was never likely to be interested in young girls.

* * *

Harry came down to breakfast the next morning to find his father had already left the table, and as Nerissa put a boiled egg in front of him he asked:

"Did we dream it last night that we have been asked to stay at Lyn?"

Nerissa laughed.

"I wondered the same when I awoke. No, it is true, but I should not count on it if I were you!"

"What do you mean by that?" Harry asked.

"I have a feeling that Delphine will somehow manage to countermand the invitation. You know she has no wish for us to know any of her friends — least of all the Duke!"

"That is true enough," Harry agreed, "but if she prevents me from going to the Horse Show, I shall strangle her!"

"Well, do not be too sure, then you will not be disappointed," Nerissa advised as she disappeared into the kitchen.

She came back with his coffee and said before he could speak:

"In any event, it is impossible for me to go. You must realise that."

"Why?" Harry asked in amazement.

"Because I have nothing to wear, and even if I spend some of the precious money Delphine gave us for last night's performance, it would be impossible for me to find anything in this part of the world which would not make me look like a peasant at one of the Duke's smart parties."

Harry looked at her in consternation.

"Are you really saying you are going to cry off?"

"I shall have to."

"But surely you can buy something with what Delphine gave you."

Nerissa smiled.

"There are much more important things I want to buy than clothes."

"What could they be?" Harry asked mockingly.

"Well, first, you are not the only person in the world who likes to ride something with four legs," Nerissa replied, "and ever since Papa's horse grew too old to carry anybody but him, I have had to walk on my own two feet."

Harry put down his cup to stare at her.

"Oh, Nerissa, I am sorry!" he said. "I did not realise how damned selfish I was being."

"I am not complaining," Nerissa said quickly, "and some of the farmers have been very kind during the hunting season in lending me their horses if they did not require them themselves. I could, in fact, have had quite a considerable stable at my disposal, until I had to close and bolt the door!"

"What do you mean?" Harry asked.

Nerissa sat down on the chair opposite him.

"You remember Jake Bridgeman?"

"Yes, of course. He runs the Posting House in the main road."

"Well, he called to see Papa one day, and after he had met me he offered me the use of his horses whenever I wished."

There was no need for Nerissa to say any more, for Harry exclaimed angrily:

"Damn his impertinence! Are you telling me he made himself unpleasant?"

"Not unpleasant ... much too pleasant, and so I had to tell him I had given up riding."

"That is not the sort of thing that should happen to you," Harry said. "If you find him being tiresome again, I will knock his head off!"

"I managed quite cleverly," Nerissa said. "Whenever I saw him come riding or driving up to the front door, I bolted it and paid no attention however loudly he knocked. You can imagine in his Study Papa never heard him, and as there are no servants except for old Mrs. Cosnet in the morning, he just had to go away."

Harry laughed at the way Nerissa spoke. Then he said:

"It is something that should not happen, but, of course, if you want a horse, dearest, I will find one for you."

"I do not intend to pay anything like as much as you will," Nerissa said. "I just want a young animal who will carry me over the fields so that I can get the exercise I sometimes long for."

"Of course you do," Harry agreed sympathetically, "and I promise you shall ride my horse when I am home, and we will take it in turns. I apologise for being so stupid as not to realise before what a rotten life you lead."

Nerissa gave a little cry.

"That is the wrong thing to say. It is not rotten! I am very happy here with Papa, and now I can afford to hire Mrs. Cosnet three, perhaps four days per week instead of two, and Papa will not only have much better food than we have been able to afford in the past, but occasionally a glass of claret at dinner. You know how much he enjoys that, and we have not had any for ages until last night."

"I was thinking after I had gone to bed that Delphine ought to do something for you. After all, you are almost nineteen, and if Mama were alive, I cannot help feeling she would have somehow contrived, because she was so clever, to have seen that you went to some Balls or received invitations at which you would meet young people of your own age."

Nerissa laughed.

"You sound like an elderly Dowager planning my marriage . . . because that is what it amounts to, does it not, Harry? That you think I ought to get married!"

"I think you ought to have the chance," Harry replied, "and what choice is there for you here in this dead-and-alive place?"

Nerissa walked round the table to put her arms round him.

"I love you," she said, "and you are not to worry about me! Just help me buy a horse that is not too expensive and I shall be the happiest person in the world!"

"I will do that," Harry promised, "but I still insist that you come with Papa and me to Lyn."

Nerissa was still wondering what she could do with her meagre wardrobe, or how she could alter some of her mother's clothes which were sadly out-of-date and far too old for her, when a groom wearing the Marquess of Sare's livery arrived with a note.

As she took it from him Nerissa knew it was from Delphine and was certain it would tell her that the invitation to Lyn had been cancelled.

Instead, she read:

I suppose we have to make the best of the mess that Papa made of everything last night, but as the Duke is determined that you and Harry should come with Papa to Lyn, I had better send you some clothes to wear.

I am returning to London first thing tomorrow morning, and will send you a trunk containing some gowns I had put to one side to dispose of to a charity, or throw away.

I am sure you will be able to alter those that need it, and at least they will look better than that old rag you were wearing last night.

58

*Tell Harry he must behave himself and make
sure he is not indiscreet in front of the Duke, otherwise he will be sorry!*

> *Yours,*
> *Delphine.*

Nerissa read it through twice.

'She is still very angry with us,' she thought, 'but
there is nothing either we or she can do about it, and at
least Harry will be grateful that the Duke still expects us
to be his guests.'

She could not help feeling that she was being treated
as a charity child, but when the trunk arrived Nerissa
could not repress the excitement she felt which was entirely feminine.

It was years since she had had a new gown, and the
moment she opened the round-topped leather box and
saw what it contained she felt her spirits rise and knew
not even Delphine could make her feel miserable at this
moment.

The gowns were all in the latest fashion and in perfect
condition, for Delphine would never wear anything that
needed even the slightest repair.

Many of her gowns she discarded after she had worn
them only once, in case those who criticised her should
recognise them again.

Nerissa was not to know that on her return to London
she had told her maid to take out of the box anything
that was at all elaborate or would, in her opinion, draw
attention to her sister.

Nevertheless, everything she had sent was in Nerissa's
eyes so beautiful and so exciting, that as she ran to try
them on, she felt as if she were dancing on air.

There were three evening gowns and day ones, a travelling dress and coat, besides what she had not dared to hope for—a very attractive riding-habit.

She thought at first there was only one trunk, but there were several smaller boxes which contained shoes, bonnets, gloves, and bags.

Even Harry had been impressed by Delphine's generosity until he read the note she had sent before leaving Sare.

Then he said:

"I am sure you would like to throw them in her face, as I would!"

Nerissa gave a little cry.

"They are mine now, and I could not bear to part with them! Although they were given grudgingly, one should never 'look a gift horse in the mouth'!"

Harry laughed and put his arm round Nerissa and unexpectedly kissed her.

"You are very sweet," he said, "and I hope one day I find for you a brother-in-law who will look after you and see that you have everything you want for yourself."

"I want nothing at the moment," Nerissa said, "except for the days to go quickly so that we can see Lyn and ride the Duke's horses."

"Amen to that!" Harry said fervently. "I am going to Oxford today to beg, borrow, or steal some decent clothes so that you will not be ashamed of me."

"Can you do that?" Nerissa asked. "Of course I would never be ashamed of you anyway!"

"When I tell the best Tailor at Oxford that I intend to spend quite a lot of money with him, I am sure he will fit me out somehow in the meantime, especially," Harry grinned, "when I tell him where I am going!"

60

Nerissa thought this an odd thing to do, but she said nothing.

She knew how much Harry resented being badly dressed when all his friends were so smart.

She found herself remembering how exquisitely tied the Duke's cravat had been the night he came to Queen's Rest, and how the points of his collar rested exactly at the right angle above his chin.

'If Harry expects to look like the Duke, he is going to be disappointed,' she thought.

Then she told herself that no one could look more attractive or be kinder and more understanding than her brother.

"Why should we answer to anyone?" she asked her reflection in the mirror.

She tilted her chin upwards in a gesture of pride that came from her Stanley antecedents.

Up to the very last moment it seemed as if they would never be ready to leave on Friday morning when the Duke's carriage arrived for them.

Nerissa guessed that the Duke would have arranged with the Marquess that his horses and their drivers could stay the night at his house so that they would not have far to come when Friday arrived.

Where Nerissa was concerned there were a million things to attend to, and she thought that in order to finish them she would have to stay up all night on Thursday.

Her father's clothes had originally come from a good Tailor, but they had, of course, deteriorated over the years.

It meant hours of sponging and pressing with hot irons to make them look even fairly respectable.

Needless to say, Marcus Stanley was not in the least

interested. All he was concerned with was to bring his chapter up-to-date so that he could put in Lyn at the last moment and miss nothing which would contribute to his whole picture of Elizabethan architecture.

When however he was dressed in his best clothes and had tied his cravat that had been ironed and pressed a dozen times to make it look new, Nerissa thought to herself that it would be difficult even for Delphine to find fault.

"You look very smart, Papa," she said aloud, and kissed his cheek.

"So do you, my dear," he said in surprise.

Because she could not help being thrilled with her own appearance, Nerissa pirouetted round the hall in front of him, displaying her muslin gown with its blue ribbons and over it a travelling cape of the same blue that was echoed in the trimming of a very expensive and attractive bonnet to match.

It was Harry who was most excited when the Duke's travelling carriage arrived and they found it was drawn by six horses.

"I expected four," he said to Nerissa in awe-struck tones.

"It is a long way to Lyn," Nerissa replied, "and I expect His Grace has no wish for us to be late."

Their luggage was disposed of in the back of the carriage and they settled themselves against the comfortable padded seat which was wide enough to hold all three of them.

"It is a good thing we are all thin!" Harry observed. "I hate travelling with my back to the horses."

"So do I," Nerissa agreed, "and it is what you used to make me do when I was small, and I doubt if you would be more polite now."

Harry laughed.

"Remember we all have to be on our best behaviour with Sister Delphine waiting to find fault. I am terrified she will be ashamed of her countrified relatives."

Nerissa knew this was the truth, and she sent up a little prayer that she would not make any mistakes.

She thought she would try to remember all the things her mother had told her about big houses and how people behaved at parties.

She felt in fact more and more apprehensive until at exactly the time the Duke had said they would arrive, the horses turned in at the huge impressive wrought-iron gates which she knew was the entrance to Lyn.

There was a long avenue of lime trees in front of them, then at the end of it she saw for the first time the house of which she had heard so much, but had never supposed she would see.

Never had she imagined that anything could be so beautiful, so fairylike, and so enormous, and yet give an unsubstantial, ethereal impression, as if it might float away into the sky at any moment.

"It is certainly large enough!" Harry remarked in awe-struck tones as they proceeded towards it.

"It is beautiful!" Nerissa exclaimed. "I only hope it does not vanish before we reach it."

Harry laughed, and as if he understood what she was saying, he pressed her hand.

"You are looking beautiful too," he said, "so cheer up and remember we are going to buy two horses when we get home again."

"That will be exciting," Nerissa said.

"There are bound to be a great number here we shall long to own," Harry murmured almost beneath his breath.

He was looking to where he could see in the distance

the arrangements that had been made for the Horse Show tomorrow.

Already there were a number of horses being walked around a miniature race-course for their riders to inspect the jumps, and there were tents and booths, which would cater for the expected crowd, and they passed them before they proceeded down the last stretch which led to the front door of Lyn.

Then as they drew up outside what seemed to Nerissa to be the most beautiful doorway she had ever seen she told herself that this was an experience of which she must remember every detail because it was something which would never happen to her again.

*   *   *

Afterwards Nerissa could only look back on a kaleidoscope of pictures which seemed to flash in front of her eyes as they passed through the Great Hall with its Minstrels' Gallery and magnificent marble fireplace and along corridors draped with tapestries.

Only then did they reach what the Butler told them was the red Library, where the Duke would be waiting for them.

After that it was difficult to remember anything except how spectacular he looked against the books that covered the walls below a ceiling which irresistibly drew Marcus Stanley's eyes upwards.

"Welcome to Lyn!" the Duke said, and to Nerissa's relief he was alone. "I hope you have had a pleasant journey."

"It was very comfortable," Marcus Stanley answered, "and thank you for the delicious luncheon that was provided for us at the Inn at which we stopped."

"I always take my own food on long journeys," the Duke said loftily. "What one usually finds at wayside Inns is quite inedible."

Before her father could answer, the Duke said to Nerissa:

"And what do you think of my house so far, Miss Stanley?"

"I am so afraid it will vanish before I have time to see it," Nerissa answered.

The Duke laughed.

Then they were shown the bedrooms which had been allotted to them so that they were near each other.

After Nerissa had been helped by two maids to change from her travelling clothes into a simple afternoon gown that was trimmed with lace run through with little velvet ribbons, they went down to where tea was waiting for them in the Long Gallery.

Here many of the Duke's house party were already assembled and amongst them of course was Delphine.

Nerissa felt her heart beat a little quicker because she was nervous as Delphine detached herself from where she was talking to two elegantly dressed young men and moved towards them to exclaim in a somewhat affected voice:

"Dearest Papa! How wonderful to see you! I do hope the journey has not been too terribly exhausting."

"Not in the slightest," Marcus Stanley replied. "As I have already assured our host, I am delighted to be here. It is even finer and more impressive than I expected it to be."

"That is how we all feel," somebody said who was listening, and there was a little ripple of laughter.

Then when she had greeted Delphine the Duke introduced Nerissa to a number of people, and while she found it impossible to remember all their names she found to her surprise that they were very friendly and, in fact, kindly.

"Is this your first visit here?" an elderly woman asked who she gathered was the Duke's aunt.

"Yes, Ma'am, and you can imagine how exciting it is for my brother and me to come to the most famous house in England."

The lady laughed.

"You must say that to our host! He appreciates compliments about his house far more than compliments about himself, which is unusual in young people these days."

"I have never had any compliments," Nerissa said without thinking, "but if they were very personal, I can imagine they would be quite embarrassing."

As she finished speaking she found the Duke was beside her and had heard what she said.

"Never had any compliments, Miss Stanley?" he enquired. "Are the gentlemen who live in your part of the world blind?"

Nerissa looked at him a little suspiciously before she said:

"That is a compliment, and a very clever one!"

The Duke laughed spontaneously.

"I can assure you that in a few years you will be quite blasé about all the flattering things that are said to you, but for the moment just enjoy them as they are and do not be too critical."

"I could never be critical about anything here," Nerissa said, "and ... please ... when may I see the whole house?"

The Duke looked at her in surprise. Then he said:

"That is a very awesome task to undertake the moment you arrive. I think I remember suggesting to your father that we leave the exploration of Lyn until after the Horse Show tomorrow."

"Yes, of course, I remember that now," Nerissa said. "It is just that everything is so beautiful, and I am so afraid I might miss something."

The Duke smiled.

"Now, that is a very ingenious compliment, Miss Stanley, and one I appreciate."

Nerissa blushed as she said:

"I am sure, Your Grace, you are so used to people eulogising over your house and everything you do that you must at times find it rather boring."

"Who told you that is what they do?" the Duke asked.

"Harry, as it happens!" she replied.

"I hope Harry is discreet in everything he tells you!"

Nerissa remembered how Harry had had a great deal to say about the Duke's love affairs, and because the Duke's question confused her she could only look away from him and feel the colour once again coming into her cheeks.

The Duke laughed softly.

"You must learn not to believe everything you hear," he said, "and to judge people for yourself."

"I try to do that," Nerissa replied. "Mama called it using one's instinct. She was always very insistent that we should never believe unkind or cruel things about people unless we were conclusively convinced that what was said was true."

"That is definitely the correct way to behave," the Duke confirmed. "I often think that people are in such a hurry that they accept other people's judgements instead of using their own, and very seldom, as you say, use their perception."

"I suppose that is difficult until one is older and wiser,"

Nerissa said, "and, of course, very much more experienced."

"That is something that will come eventually," the Duke said. "In the meantime, let me suggest that you wait for a little while and use your perception."

He moved away from her as he spoke to speak to somebody else, and she thought it was rather a strange conversation to have with the Duke of Lynchester on only the second time she had met him.

Delphine came to tell her that it was time they all went upstairs to change for dinner, and as soon as they were alone she said:

"You are not to push yourself, Nerissa! You have come to this party, which I think was a mistake, simply because the Duke was feeling kind to Papa and because he wished to please me. Therefore you will keep out of his way as much as possible!"

"Yes, of course," Nerissa said humbly.

Then as there was no maid in the room and no one to overhear, she asked:

"Has His Grace asked you yet to marry him?"

"I call that a very impertinent question," Delphine replied, "but I will pander to our curiosity by telling you it is only a question of time. That is of course the real reason why he invited you here, so that you could meet some of the members of his family and it would not be such a frightful shock when he announces his marriage to me."

"A shock?" Nerissa questioned.

"Of course it will be," Delphine replied. "Everybody has been trying to persuade the Duke to marry for years and years. He has always resisted the idea and made it quite clear that he preferred being a bachelor, and no one could influence him in any way until he was ready to present his Duchess to the world."

Delphine's voice seemed to trill on the word "Duchess."

She walked across to the mirror and said, preening herself in front of it:

"Think how lovely I shall look in a diamond tiara that is almost like a crown!" she said. "There is also one of emeralds and another of rubies, which will not be so becoming, and another of sapphires, which will definitely enhance the gold of my hair and the blue of my eyes!"

"You will look absolutely beautiful, Delphine," Nerissa said sincerely. "Will I be able to see you?"

There was a little pause before Delphine replied:

"To be truthful, I think it is unlikely. I cannot be bothered to trouble myself with relics of the past which is what a family always is. I want to meet new people, to do new things, and most of all to conquer the Social World."

"In other words, you will have no time for Harry and me," Nerissa said forlornly.

"To be honest, I think it would be a mistake, a very grave mistake, to encumber my life with either of you," Delphine said. "I have certainly done my best for you at the moment. I have brought you here, given you a lot of money, and shown you a world which I know you had no idea even existed."

It flashed through Nerissa's mind that she could point out to Delphine that none of that had been her original intention.

The money she had given them had been payment in a form of bribery so that somewhat reprehensibly they would help her to deceive the Duke into believing they lived in quite a different way from what was the truth.

Then she told herself there was no point in arguing.

Delphine even as a small child had always believed what she wanted to believe, and Nerissa was sure that she was not thinking to herself how kind and generous she had been to her poor, poverty-stricken relatives and no one could expect any more from her.

'Whatever else happens,' she thought, 'I shall have seen Lyn, and that is something I shall never forget!'

Aloud she said:

"Thank you, Delphine, for everything, and I shall try to do exactly what you want while we are here."

Delphine turned from the mirror to look at her before she said:

"What I want, quite frankly, is for you to keep away from the Duke! You are too pretty, Nerissa, for my peace of mind, so just keep out of sight...."

She paused, then added in a threatening tone of voice:

"If you do not do so, I will send you home or make you stay in this bedroom all the time you are here."

Nerissa gave a little gasp.

Then as if what she was thinking made Delphine definitely angry, she swept out of the bedroom without another word, shutting the door sharply behind her.

chapter four

NERISSA awoke early as she always did and took a minute or two to realise where she was.

Then with an irrepressible feeling of excitement she remembered that she had arranged with Harry last night that they would go riding very early in the morning.

He had taken her to one side and told her:

"The Duke has said that any time I want a horse I only have to go to the stables and ask for one. Why do you not ride with me early tomorrow morning before everybody else gets worked up about the Show?"

Nerissa's eyes lit up.

"Can we really do that?" she asked.

"There is nothing to stop us," Harry answered, "unless you oversleep."

"I shall certainly not do that if there is a chance of riding!" Nerissa replied.

She was glad to be able to get to bed early.

Everybody in the party seemed to know each other intimately and she could not help feeling out of it, first when the ladies retired to the Drawing Room, leaving the gentlemen to their port, and afterwards, when it was quite obvious that like Delphine, each one was concentrating on one particular man, and had no wish to talk to anybody else.

Most of the Duke's female guests were extremely sophisticated, beautiful women who had important titles.

They were scintillatingly dressed and their complexions were skilfully enhanced by the use of rouge and powder.

They made Nerissa feel very young and, though she was wearing what she thought was a beautiful gown belonging to Delphine, somewhat dowdy beside them.

She had chosen one that to her had seemed almost too grand for a Ball in London, but when she came downstairs, she realised the main difference between herself and the other ladies was that she had no jewellery.

The maid who was looking after her was aware of this and said to her:

"As you've no jewels, Miss, I wondered if you'd like some flowers to wear in your hair, and perhaps on your gown?"

Nerissa clasped her hands together.

"How kind of you to think of it, Mary," she said. "I do not suppose anybody will notice me, but I would not wish my own family to feel ashamed of my appearance."

"I'm sure they'd never do that, Miss," Mary replied sincerely. "There's a little bunch of white roses here which I can fix at the back of your head."

The white roses certainly enhanced her appearance, Nerissa thought, and there was another bunch of them to wear in front of the gown which she had thought when she put it on was too low to be really decent.

When she went downstairs however and saw that Delphine was wearing a sparkling necklace of diamonds and pearls with earrings to match and bracelets on each of her wrists, she felt almost conspicious by being inconspicious.

Reaching the Drawing Room, she went at once to her father's side and saw by the expression on his face that he was enjoying himself.

When Harry joined them both she knew that everything to him was a delight that had raised his spirits and made him look more handsome than usual.

But Harry had not joined her after dinner, being very busily engaged with a lovely lady glittering in sapphires who was apparently making him laugh a great deal before they moved into the room where there was dancing.

Nerissa danced once or twice, then when she thought that no one would notice, she slipped upstairs to bed.

"It has been a wonderful evening!" she told herself. "But I do not want to spoil it if people feel they have to speak to me because I am sitting or standing alone."

Now she put on the smart habit that Delphine had given her which was of a soft blue material and there was a lace-edged petticoat to wear underneath it.

Then when she had arranged her hair Nerissa thought, as it was so early in the morning and there would be nobody about, there would be no need for her to wear the elegant riding-hat that went with the habit until later in the day.

She always rode bare-headed at home, and feeling sure there would only be Harry to see her now, she felt freer and more comfortable as she was.

She opened her bedroom door quietly so as not to disturb anybody and tiptoed past her father's room knowing that Harry's was on the other side.

She did not knock but opened the door, expecting to find him nearly dressed and waiting for her.

To her surprise she saw he was still in bed fast asleep.

She was just going to wake him up when she realised he was sleeping deeply, snoring slightly, and the clothes he had worn the night before were scattered untidily over a chair and on the floor.

Nerissa looked at him for a moment.

Then she knew this meant that Harry had been very late coming to bed and also had doubtless drunk too much of the Duke's excellent wine.

Not that he would have been drunk, for Harry was far too sensible for that. But because they could never afford alcohol at home and he seldom had enough money to buy it at Oxford, it would be far more intoxicating to him than to another man of his age who was used to it.

Nerissa went a little nearer to the bed and as she looked down at her brother in the dim light coming from the sides of the drawn curtains she thought he looked very young and very vulnerable.

She decided it was important he should be at his best today of all days, when he would be seeing magnificent horses, talking to their owners about them, and hoping to please the Duke so that he would invite him to Lyn another time.

Very gently she tiptoed from the room, and closing the door went on alone down the passage.

Harry had told her the night before the way to the stables and she found it without any difficulty, only passing a few servants who looked at her in astonishment, obviously not expecting one of the guests to be about so early.

There was also, as she might have expected, not a lot of activity in the stables.

But when she finally found a groom and told him she wished to have a horse to ride, one was saddled for her immediately.

It was a spirited young bay, but at the same time had obviously been well trained, and as Nerissa was helped into the saddle she thought this was one of the most exciting moments in her life.

"If ye keep t'the right when ye get out of t'stables, Miss," the groom said, "ye'll find yer way t'some flat ground, where there's an excellent gallop."

"Thank you." Nerissa smiled, knowing the preparations for the Show were all on the left.

Slowly, knowing she had never ridden such a fine horse before, and yet aware she would have no difficulty in controlling him because he responded to every touch of the reins, she moved off.

She rode through the Park, taking care to avoid the rabbit holes under the trees, then saw ahead of her the flat ground which the groom had described.

It must be a mile long, she thought, and taking a deep breath she urged her horse forward, knowing she would go faster than she had ever ridden in her whole life.

It was thrilling to feel the soft wind in her face, and hear only the thud of hooves.

Her eyes were half-blinded by the light from the early sun, and as she flew over the ground she thought she might have stepped into one of the Fairy Tales she told herself when she was busy cleaning the house.

As she saw the end of the ride coming nearer, she

75

pulled in her horse, knowing they had both enjoyed the sensation of moving so swiftly and were both a little breathless.

When she had come to a standstill she looked back and realised there was somebody else on the ride close behind her.

She had the feeling that a few seconds more, and he would have overtaken her. As he drew up beside her, the Duke said:

"Good morning, Miss Stanley! I guessed when my groom told me there was a lady riding ahead of me that it could only be you!"

"Why should you think that?" Nerissa asked.

The Duke smiled.

"Because all my other lady guests are taking their beauty sleep."

Nerissa laughed because he made it sound so funny.

At the same time, she was vividly conscious of how magnificent he looked on his large black stallion and how elegantly dressed he was.

He had raised his hat as he spoke to her, and now as she saw him glance at her head Nerissa felt embarrassed.

"I . . . I did not think . . . anybody would be up so early," she said by way of explanation, "so I am afraid I look very . . . unconventional."

"You look very lovely," the Duke contradicted, "and as fresh as the spring!"

The way he spoke did not make her feel embarrassed because there was a dry note in his voice, almost as if he were mocking her as he said the words.

"I hope you do not . . . mind my riding one of your horses without . . . asking your permission," Nerissa went on. "But . . . Harry told me you had said he could have a horse whenever he wanted one, and I hoped that also applied to me."

"My stable is of course at your disposal," the Duke replied. "But where is Harry?"

"He was still asleep when I left and I did not want to wake him."

The Duke gave a short laugh.

"That is the penalty one pays for late nights, beautiful women, and unpredictable cards!"

Nerissa gave a little gasp. Then she said:

"You are not . . . telling me that Harry was . . . gambling last . . . night?"

There was such a note of horror in her voice that the Duke said:

"You sound as if I have shocked you!"

"It does not shock me," Nerissa answered, "but it does frighten me."

She paused for a moment, then she said:

"Please, Your Grace, do not let Harry do anything so crazy as to play cards or bet in any way. He cannot afford it!"

"Are you really so poor?"

"We are as poor as churchmice," Nerissa answered. "Harry has a little . . . a very little money at the moment, but it has to last him for years."

There was a frightened note in her voice as she thought that if Harry did anything so crazy as to throw away his money at card games, he would not be able to afford to buy a horse or the clothes he was longing to possess.

She was not aware the Duke was watching the expression on her face until he said:

"You say Harry has a little money at the moment, but I presume, since everybody has different ideas of poverty, that with such delicious food and excellent wine as you served the other evening, you are hardly on the verge of starvation!"

There was a sarcastic note in his voice which told Nerissa he thought she was putting on an act, and she said defensively:

"The night you dined at my father's house was very exceptional, Your Grace."

"In what way?"

Too late Nerissa realised this was something she should not have told him, and she wondered what she should reply.

Then, as if he had been working it out for himself, the Duke said:

"Perhaps, and you must forgive me if I am wrong, the meal you cooked so brilliantly on that particular night was provided by your sister."

The colour rose in Nerissa's cheeks, and as she looked away from him shyly he knew he had guessed right and said:

"And were your servants really taken ill?"

Nerissa was frightened.

"Please," she said, "you must not . . . ask me any . . . questions. And now that our horses are rested, could we not gallop them . . . again?"

"Of course, if that is what you wish," the Duke agreed. "But you have made me very curious, mostly, I admit, because I had no idea that you and your brother existed until you materialised in a very strange way and, now I come to think about it, in a most unlikely place!"

Nerissa was now really worried and said:

"Please . . . Your Grace . . . will you forget that we have had this conversation . . . and promise me you will not mention it to . . . Delphine."

"You sound as if you are frightened of your sister," the Duke said accusingly.

"My feelings cannot be of very much interest to Your Grace . . . one way or the other!" Nerissa replied evasively.

Feeling that everything she said was only making things worse, she touched her horse with the whip and instantly he sprang forward.

It took a second or two for the Duke to catch up with her, and then they were riding side by side back along the gallop with Nerissa striving in every way she could to outride him.

She knew it was impossible, and yet she wanted to challenge him, she wanted to prove, although she did not know why, that she was not a nonentity, but someone he must reckon with, if in no other way, at least when they were riding.

It was clear however that he was too good for her, and when finally he reined in his stallion he was half a length ahead.

At the same time it had been for Nerissa such an exciting race that her eyes were sparkling and her hair seemed to be part of the sunshine.

"I have never ridden such a wonderful horse before!" she exclaimed at last when she could get her breath. "Thank you! Thank you! It is something I shall remember and think about for ever!"

"I hope you will have many more far more exciting and perhaps more enjoyable memories than this!" the Duke remarked.

"I do not believe it!" Nerissa replied. "I only wish I could go on riding to the end of the world . . . and never stop!"

The Duke chuckled.

"I think that the pleasure of riding the most superlative horse would fade after a little while if one had nothing else in one's life."

"You say that because you have so much," Nerissa protested, "but for ordinary people, just one wonderful experience is enough to make them happy and, although you may not believe it, to fill their lives."

"Now," the Duke said, "I think, Miss Stanley, you must be talking of love. It is only love, or so I am told, that can make even the dullest and most boring life so wonderful that one needs nothing else."

"That is true," Nerissa agreed. "Mama never minded that she could not have a horse, entertain lavishly, or go to London and buy elegant gowns, because she was so happy with Papa."

"And that is what you are looking for," the Duke said as if he must tie her down to saying something positive, "a husband who will fill your life with love, and nothing else will be of any consequence."

There was a little silence as they moved away from the gallop and under the trees while Nerissa thought over what he had said.

Because he had spoken quietly and sounded sincere, she wanted to answer him in the same vein, just as she argued and discussed subjects with her father when he paid her any attention.

Now she replied quite unselfconsciously:

"I suppose, at the back of my mind, I would like to be married and have a home of my own. At the same time, it is the person with whom one shares it that matters and, as you say, nothing else is really of any importance."

She was thinking as she spoke of how Delphine had married Lord Bramwell simply because he was so rich, and had admitted the other day that she had been bored with him as a man.

"Have you any particular person in mind with whom you might like to share this *El Dorado?*"

Now the Duke sounded somewhat cynical and sarcastic again, and Nerissa laughed.

"I was really thinking, since you have brought up the subject, Your Grace, that I would like to spend my life with the gentleman I am riding. I am sure he would be far more amenable, and far more exciting to be with than any ordinary man would."

"We are not talking about an ordinary man, Miss Stanley," the Duke answered, "but somebody special with whom you are in love and who of course is in love with you."

Nerissa felt he was mocking again and she said:

"You are making me feel very . . . ignorant and rather . . . foolish to . . . talk of such things. Tell me instead about your horses and how many you possess."

"Now you are running away from what I was finding an intriguing discussion," the Duke objected.

"But somewhat one-sided," Nerissa flashed without thinking, "since you are so experienced on the subject, while I have no knowledge of it at all!"

"You have never been in love?"

"We live very quietly at Queen's Rest," Nerissa parried. "The only men who come to see Papa are very old, very learned, and they tend to concentrate on bricks and mortar rather than on women!"

The Duke laughed. Then he said:

"That is a very sad story, Miss Stanley, but at least you can make up for it by enjoying the company of a great number of men whom you will meet today."

"We have come here to look at your horses, Your Grace," Nerissa said quickly, and again the Duke laughed.

They rode back through the beautiful woods which Nerissa thought must be peopled by the gnomes, fairies, and the dragons that had filled her mind as a child.

They reached the centre of the wood, where there was a pool with irises growing around it and overshadowed by weeping-willow trees.

"I was always sure when I was a boy that this place was enchanted," the Duke said unexpectedly, and Nerissa's eyes widened in surprise before she said:

"I felt your wood was that, but then I always feel when I am among trees that they are part of a world we can reach only by stepping out of our own."

"Is that what you do often?"

"Whenever I can," Nerissa said simply, "but I do not have a great deal of time."

The Duke looked puzzled and she explained:

"Papa is very lonely since Mama died and, although he is immersed in his books, he likes to talk to me about them and to read me what he has written, and sometimes I am able to help him. There are also, unfortunately, a great number of household chores."

There was a little twist to the Duke's lips as he said:

"I was, as it happens, rather suspicious about those servants who were taken ill at the last moment, and also your friends from where you had to return because of a case of measles."

Nerissa gave a little cry.

"I asked you to forget about it," she said. "You are probing . . . and . . . prying, and it is something you must not . . . do!"

"Why not?"

"Because Delphine would be very . . ."

Nerissa stopped.

Because he had flustered her she had been about to give him the truthful answer, that Delphine would be very, very angry if she knew he had not been deceived by the charade she had made them enact for his benefit.

"Please . . ." she begged, "promise me that you will not . . . mention any of this . . . conversation to . . . Delphine."

"I thought I had given my promise already," the Duke said. "I want you to trust me, Nerissa, not to make any trouble for you or Harry in any way. It is something I should much dislike doing, and something that is in fact unnecessary."

There was a silence, then Nerissa, looking away from him, said:

"It is all rather . . . difficult, and I do want Papa and Harry to enjoy being here in this wonderful place . . . and not regret it afterwards."

"Is that what you think they will do?" the Duke enquired.

"Only if you frighten me," Nerissa answered.

"Then I promise I will do nothing to upset you, or frighten you," he said. "I want you to enjoy yourself, Nerissa, and it should not be a very difficult thing to do."

"No, of course not," Nerissa agreed, "and it is very, very kind of you to have us."

There was another silence, then the Duke said reluctantly:

"I suppose we ought to be getting back, and I dare say you are hungry."

"Now you mention it, I am looking forward to breakfast." Nerissa smiled.

They moved out from the trees and rode at a trot

through the Park and back towards the house.

As it lay ahead of them Nerissa thought nothing could be more beautiful or more ethereal.

It struck her the Duke was exactly the right person to own it, looking as he did as if he too had stepped out of a Fairy Tale.

They had not spoken for some moments, then he said:

"Are you thinking of my house?"

"Yes," she replied, "and of you."

"And what have you decided?"

"That neither is . . . real . . . that I have stepped into one of my . . . dreams and there you both are!"

The Duke laughed.

"I will accept that as one of the nicest compliments I have ever been paid, and dreams do sometimes come true."

Nerissa looked again at the house. Then she said:

"I think whoever built Lyn must have given not only his mind to it, but also his heart and soul. I feel that by no other means could it have been made so perfect, both human and Divine!"

She was speaking more to herself than to the Duke, and only when she realised he was looking at her did she feel that perhaps she had been too effusive.

"I . . . I am sorry," she said quickly, "but you did ask me what I felt."

"It is what I wanted to hear," the Duke said quietly.

They rode on without speaking until they reached the front door.

*   *   *

The Horse Show was everything that Harry had longed for, and because he had spent a long time with Nerissa inspecting the horses and watching the events take place, she was blissfully happy.

It was only towards the end of the afternoon that Delphine, who appeared to have been deliberately avoiding her sister, came up to her to say:

"Nerissa, here is somebody who is very eager to meet you, and I promised that you should be properly introduced."

Beside her stood a tall man with a somewhat Military bearing and a curly moustache, whom Nerissa had noticed the previous evening as one of the house party, and had not thought him particularly pleasant.

He had been at her end of the table at dinner, laughing rather loudly and making frequent remarks about the other guests which he signalised by lowering his voice and speaking behind his hand.

She had thought it very bad manners, the kind of behaviour her mother would have considered ill-bred.

Now Delphine was announcing his name.

"Sir Montague Hepban, and this, Montague, as you well know, is my younger sister, Nerissa."

"Whose acquaintance I am longing to make," Sir Montague said. "I had hoped to dance with you last night, but alas you vanished, and I searched in vain."

Delphine laughed.

"That sounds very unlike you, Montague," she said. "I thought you always achieved your objective."

"I do," Sir Montague replied, "but you must give me time."

Delphine moved away, and Nerissa was left with Sir Montague.

"Have you had enough of all this display of horse-flesh?" he asked, "because if so, I suggest we go and sit down somewhere quiet where I can talk to you and tell you how captivated I am by your adorable little face!"

The way he spoke seemed to Nerissa somewhat insincere and what Harry would call "slimy."

It made her decide that she definitely did not like Sir Montague, but for the rest of the afternoon he would not leave her.

It was difficult to get away, as she knew so few people, and though he spoke to almost everyone they met he did not stop, but taking her by the arm moved her through the crowds until she found they were leaving the Horse Show and walking back towards the house.

"I do not want to go in yet," she said quickly. "I am sure there are still a great many things I have not yet seen."

"We have both seen enough," Sir Montague said firmly, "and the main events are all over. As you can see, the Duke is handing out the prizes with that benign pomposity which is mandatory on such occasions."

Nerissa decided he meant this to be funny, although she thought it rather rude.

She walked on in silence, thinking it would be embarrassing to insist on returning to the crowded Show, and actually she was feeling rather hot and tired after so many hours of wandering around it.

"We will find something cool to drink at the house," Sir Montague was saying, "then if you are not tired of exhibitions, I will show you the orchids in the Conservatory. I think the flowers you wore in your hair last night found exactly the right resting place for their delicate blooms."

"When we get back I should like to go to my room and change," Nerissa said. "It has been hot this afternoon, and I shall look forward more than anything else to a cool bath this evening before dinner."

"I wish I were privileged to see you in it," Sir Montague remarked.

Nerissa stiffened.

She considered what he had just said was insulting even though she knew he was only joking.

Then she told herself it was her own fault for mentioning a bath in the first place.

"You must tell me about yourself," Sir Montague was saying. "I could not believe anyone could look so young and beautiful. You seem like Persephone bringing the spring to everyone who saw her."

As Sir Montague was speaking he had put his hand under her arm, and Nerissa told herself she disliked the touch of his fingers and the feeling that he was being too familiar.

She was forced to walk up the steps beside him into the hall. Then, when she would have gone upstairs, as she wished to do, to her own room, he drew her firmly down the passage and after they had walked a little way opened a door which she found led to a Sitting Room.

"I have already told you, Sir Montague, that I wish to change," Nerissa said.

"There is no hurry," he replied, "and I have no wish for you to leave me after I have taken so long in finding you. Come and sit down and tell me about yourself."

"There is nothing to tell," Nerissa said. "Have you known my sister for long?"

"Your sister shines like a star in the glittering world of London, and we all worship at her feet!"

"She is very beautiful."

"And so are you!"

Sir Montague drew her towards the sofa and because it was impossible to resist without struggling uncomfortably against him, Nerissa sat down.

Then he sat beside her embarrassingly close, and put his arm along the back of the sofa so that it was touching her shoulders.

As she sat bolt upright she said, hoping to divert his attention:

"I wonder if it would be possible for us to have some tea? I feel very thirsty!"

"So do I, now I think about it," Sir Montague said, "but tea will take a long time, and I am sure there is a grog tray here in his room. Our host is very generous, I am glad to say, and there is no need for his guests to be thirsty."

He rose from beside Nerissa and moved to where in the corner of the room was a table on which a tray held a number of decanters, and also a bottle of champagne in an ice cooler.

He poured out two glasses and brought them back to Nerissa.

She was wondering as he did so how she could manage to escape from him without making what she was afraid might become an uncomfortable scene.

Sir Montague sat down again and lifted his glass.

"To your lovely eyes!" he said. "And may they soon look into mine with the expression I long to see!"

Nerissa looked away from him and he said:

"That is a very sincere toast, because from the moment I saw you I knew you were what I had been looking for all my life."

"I am sure that is not true," Nerissa said. "In fact you did not pay me much attention last night, even though you did say you wanted to dance with me later."

She was actually recalling in her mind exactly the way Sir Montague had behaved at dinner.

She remembered that he had been showing off to the

lady on his right who was extremely attractive, with red hair and wearing in it a tiara of emeralds.

Afterwards, she remembered, when the gentlemen had joined the ladies, he had gone at once to the side of the same lady and had, apparently, a great deal to say to her.

Then why, Nerissa asked, was he behaving to her as he was now?

She suddenly knew the answer.

It was Delphine who had told him to keep her out of the way of the Duke! Delphine who perhaps had learned, although Nerissa was praying it as not so, that she and the Duke had ridden together early that morning.

This seemed rather a far-fetched theory, however, and she told herself it must be something she was imagining.

At the same time her intuition assured her that it was the truth, and this made her feel frightened.

She put down the glass of champagne, from which she had only taken a tiny sip, and got to her feet before Sir Montague could stop her.

"You have been very kind," she said, "but now I really must go and see if my father is back. I know he would not stay very long at the Show, as he would find it tiring, and there are several things I have to talk to him about."

"There are a lot of things I want to talk to you about," Sir Montague replied, "so I will make certain that we sit next to each other at dinner tonight and afterwards we shall dance. Or, if you prefer, I can show you parts of this house you have not yet looked at."

"Thank you, that is very kind of you," Nerissa said vaguely.

He had risen to his feet as he was talking and now as she moved towards the door he was standing in front of her.

"Before you leave, he said, "I want to tell you how

beautiful you are, and how alluring I find your lips."

Nerissa stiffened and would have taken a step backward if his arms had not gone around her.

"I have a feeling," Sir Montague said, "that you have never been kissed, and I want to be the first."

"No, no! Of course not!" Nerissa cried.

Now she was struggling against him with both her hands against his chest, but she was aware his arms were very strong, and she had the terrifying feeling that he had captured her and she would not be able to escape.

"Please . . . please . . . you must not do this!"

"You cannot stop me," Sir Montague said. "I want to kiss you, Nerissa, more than I have wanted anything for a very long time."

He held her close to him, but she was turning her head frantically from side to side.

She felt with horror that she could not escape and it was only a question of seconds before he kissed her.

"Let me go!" she cried.

Then as he pulled her still closer she screamed.

"You are mine, my little spring goddess!" Sir Montague said, and Nerissa screamed again.

Then a voice from the door, cold and icy, seemed suddenly to fill the room.

"What is going on here, and who is screaming?"

It was the Duke, and Nerissa knew she was saved.

Sir Montague's arms slackened as she fought herself free and ran towards the Duke, who was standing just inside the door looking overwhelmingly large and awe-inspiring in his riding-clothes.

Without thinking she put out her hand to hold on to him, conscious as she did so that she was trembling all over with fear.

For a moment nobody spoke, then the Duke said:

"I wondered why you left the Horse Show so early, Hepban—and Sylvia is wondering the same thing!"

"As you know, Lynchester, enough can be enough!" Sir Montague said in a somewhat effected tone.

"That is obviously what Miss Stanley is finding!" the Duke said.

At the sound of her name Nerissa, realising she was now safe from Sir Montague, knew that she had best stay no longer in the room.

She made an inarticulate little sound, and moving from the Duke's side reached the doorway and disappeared through it.

There was silence while the two men listened to the sound of her footsteps dying away in the distance. Then the Duke said:

"She is too young for your sort of games, Montague, and I suggest you leave her alone."

"Of course, if you insist," Sir Montague said. "Actually it was not my idea but Delphine Bramwell's. I think she is worried because you are looking in a different direction from the one she expected."

Sir Montague did not wait for the Duke to reply but walked from the room with a swagger—a gait he always assumed when he was embarrassed.

The Duke did not watch him go, but merely walked to the window and stood looking out for a long time.

chapter five

WHEN Nerissa came downstairs before dinner to join the party she was feeling embarrassed.

She wished she could stay in her room and not have to face the Duke again, feeling he would condemn her for being so foolish as to have gone into a Sitting Room alone with Sir Montague.

She knew she would never be able to explain how difficult it would have been to refuse without making a scene.

And yet the scene that had ensued had been worse than anything she could have anticipated, and she felt humiliated by it.

She had chosen another of Delphine's pretty gowns, this time of a pale blue gauze, and Mary had procured for her some small white orchids with touches of pink on their petals to wear in her hair.

They were so pretty that Nerissa could not help feeling it was a shame to cut them and they should have been left to grow for as long as their natural life would last.

She felt however once again that because she was wearing flowers in her hair she did not look quite so drab beside the rest of the Duke's glittering lady guests.

They were all clustered together under the chandeliers, the candlelight playing on their jewels, their lovely faces, and sparkling eyes.

Nowhere, Nerissa thought, could there be a more attractive throng of people, because all the men also looked so elegant in their high, starched muslin cravats and their black silk knee-breeches.

She moved quickly to her father's side and only as she reached him did she realise he was speaking to the Duke.

"I am sure, Your Grace," Marcus Stanley was saying, "this is one of the Elizabethan houses which during the Elizabethan era held special festivals of their own."

"I do not think I have heard that before," the Duke remarked.

"There was of course the festival which took place at the beginning of May, but there were many others," Marcus Stanley explained, "including the Festival of Fruits, which I suppose now we call the Harvest Festival, the festivals of the various Saints, and, I expect, although I am not certain, there was a Festival of Flowers."

Before the Duke could reply Delphine, who had moved to stand beside him, exclaimed:

"What a lovely idea! Why do we not have one tomorrow evening? We could all appear in the flowers we resemble."

She turned her beautiful face up to the Duke's as she

spoke, and Nerissa was certain that Delphine was visualising herself as a rose, which was what she had always said she resembled.

"It is certainly an idea," the Duke said slowly.

Now several of the other ladies who had been listening joined in to say:

"But of course! It would be spectacular, and where else could we have such a choice of flowers but from Your Grace's garden and greenhouses?"

"They are at your disposal," the Duke said, "but I must refuse to allow you to deplete my special orchids in the Conservatory."

As he spoke his eyes rested for a moment on the small orchids in Nerissa's hair, and she blushed, thinking she had no right to be wearing them.

Then Delphine protested volubly.

"Oh, Talbot," she cried, "you have always promised me I should wear your star orchids when they came into bloom, and when I looked at them yesterday they were very nearly ready to flower."

"My 'star orchids,' as you call them, are so precious," the Duke replied, "that there are experts coming from all over the country to see them, as this is the first time they have been grown in England."

"Then perhaps after all it would be a mistake to have a Festival of Flowers." Delphine pouted.

There was an outcry from all the other ladies.

"How can you be so unkind, Delphine," they complained, "as to deprive us of what would be a glorious opportunity to dress up and look very different from how we do now?"

"Besides," one of the ladies added, "I am sure our most generous host will present prizes to those he considers the most beautiful."

She gave a rather spiteful glance at Delphine as she spoke and the Duke said quickly:

"I am perfectly prepared to give a prize, but the judging will be based entirely on a secret ballot in which all the gentlemen will take part."

There was a little shriek of excitement at this and one of the gentlemen said:

"I am glad we come into this game somewhere! I was rather afraid we were to be left in the cold!"

"Your votes will be very important," the Duke assured him, "and I think we should all thank Marcus Stanley for giving us the idea of such an original entertainment."

Delphine however was still looking sulky.

"I have dreamt of wearing your special orchids, Talbot," she said, "and I cannot believe you would be so unkind as to spoil my dreams."

She spoke in a soft, intimate manner which Nerissa thought was rather embarrassing.

She therefore turned to her father to say:

"It was a clever idea of yours, Papa, and now talking about it has broken a dream I had the first night I came here."

"What was it?" Marcus Stanley asked.

"It was very vivid," Nerissa answered, "but I forgot about it in the morning because I was so excited to be going riding."

She realised her father was waiting to hear what she had to say and she went on:

"I dreamt I was in one of the rooms here in which there was a lovely young woman all dressed in white. She was crying bitterly as she took from her head a wreath, I think it was of flowers, and put it away in a cabinet that was standing near her. It seemed to me a strange thing to do. Then having shut away the wreath she put her hands up to her face and, still crying, vanished!"

As Nerissa finished speaking she realised that everybody around her was listening to what she had to say.

Then in a voice which sounded suddenly harsh and hard the Duke asked:

"Who told you that story?"

Startled, Nerissa looked at him wide-eyed, then answered:

"No one! It was only a dream!"

"You may have dreamt it, but somebody must have told you about it first!"

"No! No! Of course not!"

"I find that hard to believe," the Duke replied.

Abruptly he walked away and out of the Drawing Room, leaving Nerissa and other members of the party staring after him.

Nerissa looked at her father in consternation.

"What have I said? What have I done wrong?" she asked.

Marcus Stanley did not answer, then everybody started talking at once, no longer interested in the Duke's reaction to Nerissa's story, but in the idea of dressing up as flowers.

Only Delphine seemed to be disconcerted because the Duke had left so suddenly, and after a second or two of indecision, she too left the Drawing Room.

"I . . . do . . . not understand," Nerissa said in a low voice.

Then an elderly woman, Lady Wentworth, the Duke's Aunt, who had been acting the part of hostess at both the Horse Show and the house party, came to her side, and taking her by the hand drew her to a sofa, saying as she did so:

"I can understand, Miss Stanley, your being so bewildered at my nephew's behaviour."

"But . . . why should it be . . . wrong to speak of my . . . dream?" Nerissa asked unhappily. "I had actually forgotten about it until they were talking about . . . wreaths of flowers . . . then it came back to me."

"I understand," Lady Wentworth said, "but my nephew, Talbot, is very sensitive about the family ghost."

"Ghost?" Nerissa exclaimed.

"Most great houses have one," Lady Wentworth smiled, "but unfortunately ours is connected with a rather tiresome and alarming curse."

Nerissa's eyes were on her face as Lady Wentworth went on:

"In the reign of Charles II the Duke of those days was a very gay and raffish man like his King. He fell in love with a very beautiful, innocent girl, and they were married at her home which was somewhere near here and came to Lyn to start their honeymoon.

"The story goes, but of course I expect it has been embellished over the ages, that when they arrived here one of the Duke's past loves, a beautiful but jealous woman, was waiting for them.

"She raged at the Duke for marrying someone other than herself and told his bride that she would do everything in her power to destroy their happiness."

Nerissa made a little murmur because it seemed so unkind, but she did not speak, and Lady Wentworth went on:

"The bride rushed upstairs, leaving her husband to cope with his former love. Then feeling her happiness had already gone, she took off her wreath, hid it somewhere, and then threw herself from a top window onto the courtyard below."

Nerissa gave a little cry of horror.

"How could she do such a thing?"

"If she was broken-hearted, so was the Duke," Lady Wentworth continued, "and although eventually he married again, he was never happy. From that moment the head of the family has always been told that until the wreath of the Duchess can be found the reigning Duke will never know real happiness."

"Surely that cannot be true?" Nerissa protested.

"It does unfortunately appear to be so," Lady Wentworth said. "We all try to believe it is just coincidence, but something has always occurred to destroy happiness between the Dukes and Duchesses of Lynchester."

She paused for a moment as if she were looking back before she said:

"For instance, my father—Talbot's grandfather, appeared to be very happy until quite unexpectedly his wife ran away with one of his best friends. There was, as you can imagine, a terrible scandal, but it was hushed up and she died abroad."

Nerissa was listening with her hands clasped tightly together as Lady Wentworth went on:

"Talbot's father and mother were, we all believed, ideally happy, although it was an arranged marriage. Then when he grew older the Duke became infatuated with a young woman who lived on the estate. He spent his entire time with her, refusing to have anything to do with his wife and family. You can imagine how much his behaviour scandalised not only his relative but the whole neighbourhood!"

"Has no one tried to find the wreath I saw being placed in a cabinet?" Nerissa asked.

"Of course they have," Lady Wentworth replied, "but I think if you are wise, my dear, you will not speak of this again. I was always aware that Talbot felt very deeply about his father's behaviour, and although I am sure he is far too sensible to credit that the story of the ghost is true, it is something he would not wish to discuss."

"No . . . of course not," Nerissa agreed, "and I am sorry . . . so very sorry . . . that I should have mentioned anything so upsetting."

"You could not know about it," Lady Wentworth said, "and we must just pretend when Talbot returns that nothing untoward has occurred."

"Yes . . . of course," Nerissa murmured.

At the same time she was extremely worried that she should have quite inadvertently awoken unpleasant memories.

The whole story seemed inexplicable and far-fetched, and yet she knew from her research for her father that stories of ghosts were handed down from generation to generation, and certainly there were numerous and well-attested reports of how at least by amazing coincidence what they predicted had come true.

As Lady Wentworth had advised, when the Duke returned and dinner was announced, neither Nerissa nor anyone else mentioned the ghost again and the conversation was all about the Festival of Flowers, enlivened by sparkling witticisms exchanged between one gentleman and another.

Looking at the Duke sitting majestically at the end of the table, Nerissa thought there was a slight cloud over his face, and she wondered if anybody else had noticed it.

Delphine, who was sitting next to him, was certainly making every effort to have him forget that anything had gone wrong before dinner.

She was at her sparkling best, and everybody at that

end of the table was laughing at what she said. She seemed, Nerissa thought, to glow like a light.

After dinner, when the ladies retired to the Drawing Room, they all wanted to discuss what flowers they should wear, and Nerissa, listening, realised there was going to be quite a contest over who would represent the more popular lilies, roses, carnations, and other spectacular flowers.

Delphine was rather quiet and Nerissa realised from the look in her eyes that she was planning something very subtle which she was sure would shatter everybody else's ambitions.

Because no one was taking any notice of her, Nerissa slipped out of the Drawing Room and along the passage, thinking that she might look into some of the rooms she had not already visited in the hope of recognising the cabinet which she had seen in her dream and which would contain the lost wreath.

She could still see it quite clearly in her mind's eye.

It was not unlike quite a large number of cabinets she had noticed already at Lyn, although she had not yet had the chance of inspecting many rooms except those that the party were using.

The "Grand Tour," as she thought of it in her mind, was to come tomorrow, when the Duke had promised her father he would see all the older part of Lyn, especially the rooms that had not been altered at all down the centuries.

One thing Nerissa had learned since her arrival was that in the evening the candles were lit in every room so that there was no question of groping one's way in the dark.

Mary had told her this when she was dressing her and Nerissa had exclaimed:

"It seems very extravagant!"

"It is, Miss, candles being as expensive as they are, but then His Grace is a very rich man!"

Walking down the corridor, Nerissa peeped into first one room, then another, and although there were lacquered cabinets, French ones, some of marquetry, others inlaid with ivory and precious substances, they were none of them exactly the same as the cabinet she had seen in her dream.

Then she told herself that of course the furniture must have been moved from room to room over the ages, and the unhappy bride would have gone upstairs to her bedroom after the scene with the Duke's previous love which must have taken place downstairs.

Nerissa therefore climbed a secondary staircase and found herself on the floor where she knew there were the State Bedrooms and also the Picture Gallery.

She had already heard how beautiful this was, and her father had remarked several times during the day when they were looking at the horses how much he was looking forward to seeing the Duke's pictures.

The Gallery was long, with crystal chandeliers running the whole length of it, and also silver sconces on the walls, which held lighted candles.

Fascinated, Nerissa admired several magnificent van Dycks before she came to some portraits of beautiful women painted by Sir Peter Lely at what she knew was the time of Charles II.

This, she thought, was where she might see the face of the unhappy bride of her dream.

Then she wondered whether, since she had only just become the Duchess of Lynchester, there would have been time for her to be painted.

She stood in front of one picture trying to see any

resemblance of the weeping bride whom she had watched taking her wreath from her hair.

But her instinct rather than her eye told her that the pictured face was not the same.

Then as she moved along to the next picture she heard footsteps coming down the Gallery towards her.

She turned with a startled leap of her heart to see that it was the Duke.

Feeling rather like a child who had been caught in some misdemeanour, Nerissa waited, her hands clasped together, her heart beating frantically in her breast.

As he came nearer the Duke was looking grave, and when he reached her he did not speak but stood looking down at her frightened eyes raised to him.

After a moment she said:

"I . . . I am sorry . . . very sorry!"

"For being here?" he questioned. "You need not apologise."

"N-no . . . not that . . . but because . . . I upset you . . . I did not mean to . . . do so."

"I know that."

There was a pause while they stood and looked at each other. Then he said:

"Do you really swear by everything you hold holy that nobody had told you the story of my ancestor's bride, or what occurred on their wedding day?"

"I swear it!" Nerissa said. "It was . . . just a dream . . . and I did not think it had any particular significance."

"And now you have come here to see if you can find the picture of the woman you saw in your dream!"

"Perhaps it is something I should not have done," Nerissa said, "if it makes you . . . angry."

"I am not in the least angry," the Duke replied, "only

very intrigued, and of course I want to know if you have found the face you are seeking."

Nerissa shook her head.

"Not so far," she said, "and actually I was thinking that it is unlikely she would have been painted before she was the Duchess."

"I thought that myself."

"But it was worth making certain she was not here amongst the other beautiful Duchesses of Lynchester."

There was a pause before he replied almost as if he were reluctant to say the words:

"I suppose, in that case, we should look for the cabinet. But the wreath has been searched for by, I expect, every generation of my family, and they have always been disappointed."

Nerissa looked away from him. Then after a minute she said:

"You may perhaps . . . think it . . . impertinent of me perhaps . . . I am . . . intruding on something that does not concern me . . . but I cannot help feeling there must be a reason . . . why I had that dream."

"Do you think a poor little ghost from the past was trying to get in touch with you?"

There was a sarcastic note in the Duke's voice which told Nerissa only too clearly that he did not think there was the remotest possibility of that happening.

"Will you tell me something?" she asked. "Do the stories relate exactly what happened when the Duke realised his bride had killed herself?"

"There are various versions of what took place," the Duke replied. "One is that he was so utterly and completely distraught that he never came back here again. Another is that, feeling that he could not live without the woman he loved, he also killed himself."

There was silence while Nerissa thought over what he had said. Then slowly and quietly she said:

"Do you think perhaps the Duchess regretted the curse that her action put on the family which was quite unjustified because the Duke truly loved her? Would she not try to make reparation by telling somebody to find her wreath?"

She was working it out for herself and the Duke said quickly:

"In that case she has certainly not come to me, Nerissa, but to you. So it is obvious that the only person who can remove the curse, if that is what it is, is you!"

Nerissa drew in her breath.

"That is a very frightening thought, if I am . . . unable to . . . find it."

She sounded so perturbed that the Duke said in a different tone of voice:

"I think you must be sensible about this. I cannot believe that after all these years the wreath has not crumbled to dust if it was made of real flowers, or been stolen, or even inadvertently thrown away. A dozen things might have happened to it."

Nerissa did not answer and after a moment he said:

"Forget ghosts and all spooky things which I am certain exist only in the imagination of those who have nothing else to think about! Come back to the party who are intent on playing Charades, which will amuse those who act in them more than those who watch."

"You must go back, Your Grace," Nerissa replied, "but I would like, with your permission, to look into the State Rooms which I know are on this floor."

"If that is what you want, then I will come with you," the Duke said.

They walked down the Picture Gallery and out into the corridor, and the Duke opened one of the tall doors, saying as he did so:

"This is known as the King's Room because Charles II slept here, and I think, although I am not sure, that it is very much the same as it was in those days."

It was certainly a very impressive room, with an exquisitely painted ceiling, a bed draped in silk curtains, and with furniture which Nerissa might have expected to find at Lyn.

There were two portraits on the wall, but neither of them depicted the face she wanted to see.

The Duke, with a faintly cynical smile, as if he thought the whole idea of finding anything quite absurd, opened the communicating door into the room that adjoined it.

"This is the Duchess's Room," he said, "which has been used by every Duchess of Lynchester. However, I must tell you it has been altered considerably, first by my grandmother, then by my mother, and I am quite certain not one piece of the original furnishings is to be found here."

It was in fact the most beautiful room Nerissa had ever seen, and the brocade on the walls echoed the blue sky behind the Goddess Aphrodite on the ceiling, where she was portrayed surrounded by cupids and doves.

There were also cupids on the blue canopied bed and cupids used as sconces on the walls.

It flashed through her mind that it was a room made for love.

Then as she felt a little shy at thinking such a thing, she looked towards the Duke, and realising he was watching her, felt the blood rise in her cheeks.

"I thought you would think this room beautiful," he said. "It will not be used until I bring home a bride."

'That will be Delphine,' Nerissa thought, but she did not of course say so aloud.

She only felt a strange feeling of protectiveness towards the Duke, as if she feared Delphine might hurt him and she wanted to save him from any unhappiness.

Abruptly, as if the Duke did not wish to say any more about his future marriage, he opened yet another door which led into the *Boudoir* that was connected with the Duchess's Room.

Here again there was every suggestion of love in the Fragonard pictures of lovers in a garden, cupids flying over their heads, and cupids painted by Boucher.

This room also was in the pale blue colour of Delphine's eyes, with touches of pink which seemed like rays of sunshine.

Nerissa glanced round the room at the inlaid French furniture, at the Louis XIV gilt chairs, and a satinwood commode with huge ormulu handles.

Again the Duke said in the same tone he had used before:

"I am sure you will not find what you are seeking."

It was almost, Nerissa thought, as if he were pleased to prove her wrong and to justify his assertion that there was nothing substantial or logical about ghost stories, wherever they came from.

"There are several more State Rooms to be seen," he said, "but I suggest we leave those until tomorrow, and by that time I hope the family ghost will have ceased to worry you, Nerissa."

It was the second time he had called her by her Christian name and Nerissa thought it was rather strange, and yet it seemed to come naturally to his lips.

"It will not worry me," she replied, "but I have a

feeling that although you are fighting against it, it worries you."

"Why should you think that?" the Duke asked sharply.

"Perhaps because you are more sensitive than most men about such things . . ." she began.

"And why should you think that?" he interrupted. "Who said I was sensitive?"

He spoke crossly and Nerissa gave a little cry.

"Now I have upset you, and I did not mean to do that! You have been so kind, and I have not yet thanked you for saving me from Sir Montague."

"He had no business to behave as he did!" the Duke said. "At the same time, it was not very clever of you to go back from the Horse Show alone with him and allow him to take you into an empty room."

"I know," Nerissa said unhappily, "but it just happened, I . . . I did not . . . want to make a scene about it."

"Promise me it is something you will not do again," the Duke said.

"I promise . . . and I know it was . . . very foolish of me."

She sounded so contrite that the Duke smiled.

"And now," he said, "unless you are prepared to cause endless gossip, we must return to the others."

"Yes . . . of course," she agreed.

They walked towards the door at the other end of the room.

The Duke opened it and Nerissa saw that they were in a small Dressing Room, or what she guessed had originally been intended as a Powder Room, where women could have their hair powdered without making a mess.

There was only one candle affixed to the dressing table which held a mirror in a heart-shaped frame with

107

two cupids surmounting it holding up a crown.

Nerissa gave an appreciative glance as the Duke opened the door into the corridor.

As he did so she noticed that the only other piece of furniture in the small room was a cabinet.

It was of dark wood inlaid with small pieces of mother-of-pearl and coral.

She would have passed it without taking a second look if some instinct or perception within her had not made her stop.

It was almost as if the chest was speaking to her, and as she stood still the Duke, holding the door into the passage, asked:

"What is it?"

"I believe," Nerissa said in a very small voice, "that this is the ... cabinet I saw in my dream!"

For a moment she thought the Duke was going to argue with her.

Then he came back, allowing the door to close behind him.

"How can you be so sure?" he asked.

"I ... feel it!" she replied simply.

"It must have been searched a thousand times," he said, "because it has always been in the Duchess's Suite."

"It is the chest in which she ... hid the wreath," Nerissa protested. "I am certain of it."

As if he were prepared to humour her, while at the same time thinking it was a waste of time, the Duke lit a second candle on the other side of the mirror from the one that was already alight.

Then as Nerissa stood in front of the cabinet, she found herself involuntarily praying that the unhappy bride of long ago would help her to find what she sought.

"The doors in the front open," the Duke said as if he

were prompting her to make some movement, "and I am sure they are not locked."

Nerissa remembered that in her dream no door had been opened. The bride had put her wreath in something higher up, like a drawer above the doors of the cabinet.

But when she looked there was no drawer there, just the smoothness of polished wood which curved so that it jutted slightly over the two doors beneath it and was obviously just the top of the cabinet.

Frantically she wondered if some part of the cabinet had been remodelled at some time.

The Duke did not speak as she put out her fingers to touch the carved dark lacquered wood, feeling along it to see if it moved, but finding there was nothing to suggest that it was a possibility.

Then still praying, still striving to reach the Duchess who had died so tragically so many years earlier, she ran her fingers beneath the curved surface where it protruded above the doors, finding that too smooth and without a join of any sort.

Then as she reached the end at the corner of the cabinet she was aware of a slight projection against the tip of her forefinger and she pressed it.

As she did so she felt a slight movement and she pressed it harder.

Then the whole top of the cabinet moved forward, and as it did so Nerissa saw inside a shallow and thin drawer where there lay what she recognised must be the wreath she sought.

For a moment she could not believe her own eyes. Then the Duke was beside her, holding the candle high above his head so that they could see more clearly what the drawer contained.

"It is the wreath!" he exclaimed. "How could you

possibly have known? How could you have found it after all these years?"

Nerissa could not answer, she only felt as if for a moment she had stepped into another world, another time, and it was impossible to return.

Then the Duke put the candle on top of the cabinet, and putting his hand into the drawer drew out what they had been seeking.

It was not, as Nerissa had expected, of artificial orange blossoms, but of flowers fashioned in diamonds and pearls. It was small, delicately made, and very beautiful.

As the Duke held it up to the light of the candle she felt as if, as it glittered, it spoke to her and told her from now on the curse had ended and the Dukes and Duchesses of Lynchester would remain happy until their lives ended.

The Duke was staring first in disbelief at the wreath, then at Nerissa.

"How could you have known? How could you have possibly been aware of what has defeated many generations of my family who have searched for this either because they believed in its existence, or because they wished to prove the whole story was a lot of nonsense?"

"Because it is there . . . it must be true."

"Of course it is true," the Duke said, "and now the unhappy bride can rest quietly and no longer haunt us. The only difficulty is, Nerissa, how I can thank you."

As if she suddenly came back to earth, Nerissa put up her hand and said:

"Please . . . please . . . do not tell them . . . downstairs. They will not understand . . . and I do not want to talk about it."

"But I do understand," the Duke said in his deep voice. "So I think what we will do is to put the wreath back in the place that has kept it safely for so many years. Then tomorrow we will come here together and make sure that what we have found is true and not a dream."

"That is what I would ... like to do ... Your Grace," Nerissa said, "and ... please ... you will not tell Delphine?"

"No, of course not!" the Duke said firmly. "I have already given you my word about that, Nerissa, and I will not break it."

Nerissa drew a deep breath. Then she said:

"I am glad ... so very glad ... that I have been able to help you."

"Perhaps more than you realise," the Duke said, "but again, we will talk about it tomorrow."

He put the wreath back into the drawer, then as he closed it he said with a smile:

"I suppose you can remember how to open it?"

"There must be a secret catch just at the corner, and so skilfully made that no one has been aware of it who has not been told where to find it."

"Nobody has told you, and yet you found it!"

Nerissa did not answer.

She was thinking that somehow she had been meant to find it, that was why the Duchess who had hidden the wreath had, in some strange way she could not understand, guided her fingers to find the catch.

"All that matters," she said aloud, "is that it has been found, and now when you marry, Your Grace, you will be happy."

"That is what I want to be," the Duke said.

His eyes met Nerissa's in the candlelight and for a moment it was impossible for either of them to look away.

Then with what was an obvious effort the Duke turned and put the candle back in the place from which he had taken it beside the mirror.

While he was doing this, Nerissa opened the door and stepped out into the corridor.

As she did so she felt as if she were stepping out of a dream into reality.

And yet she had no desire to return.

She wanted to stay, feeling again the strange intuition which had made her so certain that the cabinet was the one she sought.

She wanted too, although she knew it was something she should not admit, to stay with the Duke.

chapter six

SOMETHING was wrong, and Nerissa was not certain what it was.

She had thought after the excitement of last night that this would be such a happy day, and she awoke feeling that her heart was singing and all was right with the world.

She had arranged with Harry that they would ride early, before anybody else was about, and he was waiting for her when she came from her bedroom, and they went to the stables together.

They took their horses immediately to the gallop and Nerissa could not help continually looking behind, expecting every moment that the Duke would join them.

But although they stayed on the gallop for a long time there was no sign of him, and as they rode home through the woods the same way that he had taken Nerissa the first morning, she wondered why he had stayed away, and if there was some special reason for it.

Then she told herself she was being ridiculous.

Perhaps the Duke was tired after going to bed very late last night, or perhaps he had thought it would be indiscreet to be with her again early in the morning.

She wondered if Delphine had learned about it and had reproached him.

There were all sorts of possibilities, but none of them made her feel any happier.

She had not even seen the Duke when after breakfast she went to Church, it being Sunday, with his Aunt, Lady Wentworth.

When they left, none of the other ladies of the house party had yet appeared, although there were a number of men still in the Breakfast Room.

Nerissa had thought perhaps her father would come to the Church with them, but she found him in one of the Sitting Rooms busy making notes on what he had seen so far at Lyn and what he particularly wanted to examine later that morning.

"You have not forgotten," he said, "that the Duke has arranged for us to inspect the house, and I know he also arranged for his Curator to accompany us and his assistant who is also very knowledgeable on the Elizabethan period."

Nerissa thought it was foolish of her, but she had somehow expected the Duke to show them round alone, and although when the time came he had begun the tour with the Curator, after they had visited only two of the important rooms he was called away and did not return.

Nerissa tried very hard to concentrate on the Elizabethan features that were unique to Lyn.

Yet she found herself wondering if the Duke was talking and laughing with Delphine, and whether she would have the chance of going with him to see the wreath as he had promised.

It was something she was looking forward to while her father still went from room to room asking questions and making notes of the answers.

He was, she knew, blissfully happy to be seeing for himself the wonders of a house which he had always admired.

At luncheon nobody talked about anything but the Festival of Flowers which was to be held that evening.

The ladies were all being very mysterious about what they were going to wear, but Nerissa was quite certain that Delphine intended to be the winner and had planned something particularly spectacular.

She had made sure, she told them, that the judging would be taken very seriously, and the contestants, of whom there were twelve, were to walk down the steps of the dais in the Ball Room, one by one.

"We shall be accompanied by music," Delphine said, "and after all the excitement is over and the prizes have been presented, then we will dance. The Duke has asked a number of neighbours to join us, and I doubt if the Festival of Flowers at Lyn will finish before dawn."

She was making it quite clear that it was her idea and her party, and Nerissa thought she was already assuming her position as Duchess and taking up her duties.

The plans were still being discussed at teatime and she waited in vain for the Duke to give her a sign that they could go together to the cabinet and look again at the wreath that she had found for him.

It seemed so incredible that she had been able to find it that Nerissa kept wondering if she had dreamt the whole thing, and if when she went back to the Duchess's Suite she would find it impossible to open the secret drawer and would have to realise that the diamond wreath of flowers existed only in her imagination.

She was so busy with her father that it was only when she went up to wash her hands before tea that she found Mary waiting for her agitatedly.

"I wondered what'd happened to you, Miss! The gardeners told me you're the only lady as hasn't yet chosen her flowers."

"I doubt if there are any left by now." Nerissa smiled.

"That's the truth, Miss, and the gardeners are very perturbed at what little they have to offer you."

"Where are they, Mary?" Nerissa asked.

"There's only one young one left, Miss. The others have gone to make the wreaths and all the other paraphernalia the ladies have asked of them. You can't imagine how fantastic they'll look, just like something out of a Play House!"

"My needs are very simple," Nerissa said.

But because Mary pressed her, she went down the passage to where there was a young gardener waiting in a room which had been set aside for the flowers.

As Mary had told her, there was practically nothing left. The gardeners had brought sample bunches of what was available, and every lady had fought to get her own favourite flower and make sure there was enough to ornament not only her head but also her gown.

"I am sorry to keep you waiting," Nerissa said in her quiet voice.

"Tha's all right, Miss," the gardener replied. "Oi'm jus' worrit as to what Oi've to offer ye."

Nerissa looked round and was not surprised to find there were no roses, lilies, or camelias, either white or pink.

They had all been bespoken, and there was, in fact, only a small bunch of pansies of not particularly pretty colour, asters that looked somehow too hard for a wreath, and a few yellow irises which Nerissa knew would not look at all effective against the pale gold of her hair.

"Oi'm afraid that's all," the gardener said apologetically, "unless you'd consider some o' the field flowers."

Nerissa's eyes lit up.

"Have you any forget-me-nots?" she asked.

"There's 'undreds o' they, Miss. They grows loik weeds in one part o' the garden, an' we can't get rid o' them."

"Then perhaps you would be very kind and make me a wreath of forget-me-nots," Nerissa said. "I have always thought them a very beautiful little flower."

"You'll want more than a wreath, Miss," Mary said from the doorway.

Nerissa had not realised that Mary had followed her, and she turned with a smile as the young maid came into the room to say good night.

"You bring me bunches of forget-me-nots and I'll arrange them, and don't be skimpy."

"Oi'll not do that," the gardener promised.

Having thanked him, Nerissa went back to her bedroom.

"What are you planning, Mary?" she asked as she washed her hands. "I am quite happy to be unobtrusive, and I am sure my sister will win the prize and look very beautiful."

"Her Ladyship's demanded enough roses for a Coronation!" Mary exclaimed. "The head gardener's grumbling because they're his favourite pale pink and he says if Her Ladyship has everything she wants, there won't be nothing left in the garden!"

Nerissa laughed and did not worry anymore about her

appearance at the Festival of Flowers.

At the same time it gave her a warming feeling that she and the Duke shared the secret of the wreath which was far more important than anything the gardeners could provide or his other guests could wear.

But when evening came and she had still had no word from him that they should go together to the Duchess's Suite she suddenly felt depressed and spontaneously said to her father:

"Now you have seen the house, Papa, would it not be best if we leave tomorrow? I believe some of the guests who came only for the Horse Show are returning to London."

"Leave tomorrow?" Marcus Stanley echoed in amazement. "I have no intention of doing anything of the sort! I have not yet seen all the house or any of the outside buildings. The Riding School is, I am told, without its peer anywhere in the country, and the dovecotes are different from those elsewhere and so are some of the other outbuildings."

He did not wait for Nerissa to say anything, but merely remarked as he left the room:

"We will leave on Wednesday, and that will be too soon for me!"

"It was stupid of me to suggest such a thing," Nerissa told herself.

She went to her bedroom to find that Mary had already arranged what she should wear that evening.

She had herself thought that a very pale blue gown which had belonged to Delphine was the most suitable, but Mary insisted that she wanted her to wear white and she was to change into it, as the other ladies were doing, after dinner.

"Do you mean we all have to change again after dinner before we appear wearing the flowers?"

Mary smiled.

"You'll see what I mean, Miss, when they start parading 'emselves. It would be impossible for most of them to sit down to the table!"

Nerissa thought it strange, but at Mary's insistence she put on the very pretty gown she had not worn previously and went down to dinner, knowing that what she really wanted was to see the Duke.

She wondered what he had been doing all day and guessed he had spent his time with Delphine, who was looking exceedingly beautiful, glittering with jewels, and with an expression on her face which Nerissa knew meant she was very sure of her own success.

When dinner was over and they had come out of the Dining Room, Delphine immediately took charge.

"Now, hurry everyone," she said, "you know what we have to do: We all meet in the anteroom of the Ball Room without any of the other guests seeing us, and as soon as our audience is assembled, we parade through the door onto the dais and walk down the steps into the centre of the room to take our places on one side of it until we are all assembled."

Although the other ladies had apparently heard all this before, it was new to Nerissa, and she hoped she would not make any mistakes.

She went upstairs to her room to find that Mary was waiting for her, and when she saw the gown she was to wear she exclaimed in surprise.

It was a very pretty white gown of Delphine's, simple and unadorned, but now the hem was ornamented with bunches of forget-me-nots and when she had it on, Nerissa found that she had a wide blue ribbon, almost like the Order of the Garter, ornamented with tiny bunches of the same flowers to wear across one shoulder ending below her waist in a large bunch of them.

It was very effective, she thought, and so was the wreath that encircled her fair hair.

"You have taken a lot of trouble, Mary," she said, "and I think it is very kind of you."

"It may not be anything like as spectacular as what some of the other ladies is wearing, Miss," Mary said, "but in my opinion, you'll be the most beautiful of them all!"

Nerissa laughed.

"Thank you. Now you have given me confidence," she said. "But the forget-me-not is a very small, unobtrusive little flower."

When she joined the others in the anteroom to the Ball Room she realised that was certainly the truth.

Delphine looked fantastic.

She had an enormous hooped gown covered completely with pink roses and a wreath round her head. She also carried a sunshade covered in roses.

As if that was not enough, in the wreath some of her more spectacular diamonds were arranged between the flowers, and the arrangements round her décolletage was the same.

She looked sensational and so beautiful that Nerissa thought it would be impossible for anyone to rival her, which was quite obviously what Delphine thought herself.

Some of the ladies had certainly tried their best.

One, representing a lily, wore a simple white gown which had huge wings made of lilies tied to her shoulders and she carried a great sheath of them in her hands.

Another wearing red carnations had a muff of the same scented flowers, which also ornamented the hem of her white gown, and her wreath was the size of a Russian's fur hat and very attractive.

As Nerissa expected, after a brief glance no one paid very much attention to her.

Then as the music from the Ball Room grew louder Delphine said from the doorway:

"Now everybody is assembled and the judges are all in position with pencils and paper to put down how many marks they give us, as we go on. Do not forget that you have to describe your flower in either your own words or those of some Poet."

As she spoke Nerissa remembered that she had been surprised when she came into the anteroom to see one or two ladies looking through books of what appeared to be poetry.

She supposed she had not listened very carefully, or else had not been told that she was to describe her flower.

Quickly she tried to remember if she had ever known of some famous Poet like Lord Byron writing of anyting so insignificant as a forget-me-not.

There was what sounded like a roll of drums and as Delphine, holding her small sunshade over her head, swept through the door onto the dais, there was a loud burst of applause.

Nerissa realised that the guests whom the Duke had invited to join them after dinner must have already arrived, and from the sound of the applause she knew they had quite a large audience waiting for them.

One by one the ladies left the anteroom and were moving as if they had had years of practice.

As they entered the Ball Room Nerissa could hear each of them saying a few words in clear, unhesitating tones before the music grew louder and then, she thought, they must be walking to their places, as Delphine had commanded.

As eleven contestants left in front of her, she realised with a faint little smile that she was the last because she had made no effort to have herself placed anywhere else.

She reached the doorway, waited until she knew the last lady, resplendent as a white camelia, had reached her appointed place, then she moved slowly forward.

For a moment the lights in the Ball Room were so bright that she felt dazzled by them, and she also unexpectedly felt shy.

Then she knew that while everybody else was just a sea of faces, she saw the Duke seated amongst the other gentlemen who were all judges.

She knew then she could not shame herself in front of him.

Gracefully she walked to the front of the stage, and without having to think of it, some lines came to her lips and she said them in a soft, very sweet voice that somehow compelled everybody to listen to her.

The forget-me-not—blue as the sky,

Small, unnoticed—which is why

You will forget with somebody new

But I will always remember you.

122

As she finished speaking the applause rang out and she walked down the steps with her eyes lowered to join the other contestants.

She realised that all grouped together they formed a bouquet and then as the audience clapped and went on clapping, the Duke collected the voting papers and going onto the platform made a short speech.

He said he was sure this Festival of Flowers had been more impressive than any festival that had ever taken place before at Lyn and that certainly nothing could be more beautiful than the human flowers that graced the Ball Room.

Then he read out the result of the voting and it was not surprising that Delphine came first.

'That will make her happy!' Nerissa thought.

She did not miss the satisfaction on her sister's face as she moved towards the Duke to receive from him the First Prize which was a very charming brooch in the shape of a flower made of enamel and set with small semi-precious stones.

Nerissa was near enough to hear her say "Thank you" in a voice that everybody in the Ball Room could hear, and then in a whisper that was meant only for the Duke:

"You know I shall treasure this because you have given it to me."

There was an intimate note in her voice and an expression in her eyes that the Duke could not misunderstand.

But Nerissa thought he made no response, and Delphine was obliged to move away to make room for the Lily who had won the Second Prize.

As soon as the prize-giving was over, everybody in the Ball Room surged forward wanting to look at the Beauties more closely and to ask them, although in some cases it would be a difficult manoeuvre, for a dance.

Nerissa went to find her father but it was obvious he did not wish to be interrupted, engrossed as he was in conversation with a gentleman who owned a house not far from Lyn which was also of the Tudor period.

Nerissa was therefore glad when Harry approached to slip his arm through hers and say:

"You look smashing! I thought the forget-me-nots very appropriate."

"Why?" Nerissa asked.

"Because we shall certainly, none of us, ever forget being here, and I have something to tell you."

He drew her away from the noise into another room and she asked apprehensively:

"What is it?"

"You will hardly believe it," Harry said, "but the Duke asked me if I had any horses. When I said no he said he would give me one which I could have with me at Oxford!"

"Did he really say that?" Nerissa cried. "How wonderful, Harry! That means you can save your money and spend it on something else."

"For a moment I could hardly believe what I was hearing," Harry said, "but now I know why he gave it to me."

"Why?" Nerissa asked.

"It is obvious! Although I would have bet against it, he has made up his mind to marry Delphine and is ingratiating himself in the correct manner with her relatives!"

"Yes...of course...that must be the...explanation!" Nerissa agreed, and wondered why she did not feel as pleased as she knew she ought to on learning that Harry was receiving such a generous gift.

For some reason the evening seemed to drag, and although she danced with quite a number of the gentlemen and managed to avoid Sir Montague, she knew she was not really enjoying herself.

'I must be tired,' she thought, and knew no one would notice if she slipped away to bed.

Delphine, obviously the Queen of the proceedings, was being fêted and complimented.

She had so many would-be partners dancing attendance upon her that she found herself taking each gentleman twice round the Ball Room before she left him for another.

"I will go to bed," Nerissa decided.

She walked up the stairs and when she would have gone to her bedroom she had a sudden longing to see the wreath and make quite certain it was still there.

She walked passed the State Bedrooms until she found the Duchess's Room, and opened the little Dressing Room door.

Everything was just as she and the Duke had left it last night.

Two candles were burning on either side of the mirror, and because the room was so small it was easy to see the cabinet quite clearly.

Nerissa looked at it, feeling as if the unhappy Duchess who had thrown away her life so unnecessarily was beside her.

"Why could you not have had faith in him?" Nerissa wanted to ask her, and she felt as if the Duchess were trying to tell her something.

She could not think what it could be, and instinctively she put out her hand and ran her fingers as she had last night along the underside of the polished top.

She found the slight protuberance at the corner that

125

she had pressed before and for a moment, as nothing immediately happened, she thought frantically that the whole thing had been an illusion.

Then slowly the drawer opened and there it was— the wreath that had lain there for so many years, carrying with it the curse which had made each Duke, one after the other, unhappy.

Nerissa reached out and drew the wreath from its hiding place.

Now, as she looked at it a little more calmly than she had last night in the excitement of the moment, she thought it was even more beautiful than she had thought at first.

The workmanship was fantastic and she guessed it must have been a foreign jeweller, perhaps an Italian, who had made it so skilfully.

She held it nearer to the candlelight on the dressing table, then on an impulse she took off her wreath made of forget-me-nots and lifting the diamond wreath in both hands set it on her head.

It seemed to fix exactly.

As she put it on she thought she heard a soft sigh beside her, as if the Duchess's ghost were satisfied and this was what she wanted.

It was only a faint impression, and yet Nerissa was certain that she had actually heard a sound and that the unhappy Duchess had been with her.

Then she was just as certain that the ghost had gone and she was alone.

It was all so strange and bewildering and yet she was convinced that she was not imaginging anything, but what she felt had actually happened.

Then as she looked at her reflection in the mirror the door of the Dressing Room opened and the Duke came in.

She could see him reflected in the mirror, but she did not turn and only watched him as he came nearer until he stood just behind her.

Now their faces were reflected side by side in front of them.

"That is how I want to see you..." the Duke said very quietly.

As if she had been awoken from a dream, Nerissa realised that he was flesh and blood, and that perhaps it was reprehensible of her to have tried on the Duchess's wreath without asking him first.

She turned quickly to apologise, then as she met his eyes she found herself unable to speak, but only to stare at him as he finished the sentence quietly:

"... when we are married!"

Nerissa's eyes widened until they filled her face.

"I knew I should find you here," he continued, "and I was in fact intending to ask you to put on the wreath so that I could see you as I am seeing you now, looking exactly as you should as my wife."

"I...I do not...know what you are...saying," Nerissa whispered.

"I am saying," the Duke said very quietly, "that I love you, and the reason why I have never married is that I have never found anyone until now who could assure me that the curse was lifted and I could now find the happiness I need in my life."

Because it seemed impossible this was happening, Nerissa could only stare at him.

Then slowly he put his arms around her and drew her against him.

"I love you!" he said, and his lips were on hers.

As he kissed her she knew that the reason why she had been unhappy and restless and everything had seemed wrong was simply that she loved him.

She had known it, but dared not express it even to herself. She had loved him, she thought wildly, from the first moment he had come into the kitchen and she thought he was the most handsome man she had ever seen.

Although she told herself he belonged to Delphine, she had found herself irresistibly drawn towards him.

From the moment they had ridden together in the early morning she had known that when he was not there the world was empty and her whole being was crying out for him.

The Duke's kiss was at first very soft and gentle, as if he were afraid of frightening her.

Then as the softness and innocence of her lips excited him, his became more possessive, more insistent, more demanding.

He kissed her until Nerissa felt as if he carried her into the sky and they were no longer human, but one with the stars.

They were a part of each other so that they were indivisible and it would be impossible for them to be separated.

Then as the Duke tightened his arms about her and went on kissing her she felt a rapture within herself that was something she had never known and was not even aware existed.

It was quite perfect, part of the magic she had felt in the woods ever since she was a child, and combined with it was the beauty of Lyn.

It merged with the Duke himself until there was nothing in the world but him. His arms, his lips, and the love that she could feel coming from him to join the love which came from within herself.

Only when the Duke raised his head did Nerissa look

up at him to say in a voice that did not seem like her own and came from a long distance away:

"I . . . love . . . you!"

"That is what I wanted you to say," the Duke said, "and I love you!"

Then he was kissing her again, kissing her demandingly, passionately, as if he had been afraid he would never find her, and now that he had, was making sure she was his.

Only when they were both breathless and Nerissa with a little murmur hid her face against the Duke's shoulder did he say in a voice that was curiously unsteady:

"How soon will you marry me, my darling?"

It was then that Nerissa came back to reality and looked up at him to say:

"A-am . . . I . . . dreaming . . . or did you . . . really ask me to . . . marry you?"

"How could I want to do anything else," the Duke asked, "when you have been given by a power I do not understand the key to our happiness—the wreath which has wrecked so many of my ancestors' lives?"

"It was so wonderful that I . . . could do that," Nerissa said, "but . . . you know I cannot . . . marry you."

The Duke's arms tightened.

"What do you mean—you cannot marry me?"

"You . . . are to . . . marry Delphine!"

The Duke shook his head.

"I have never proposed marriage to your sister, and I have no intention of doing so."

"But . . . she thought . . ." Nerissa began.

"I know what she thought," the Duke said, "and what several other women have thought before her, but I was determined, Nerissa, never to marry anybody unless I could be certain I would find happiness."

He paused for a moment before he said:

"I am not certain whether I really believed in the curse or not, but I knew, what you would call perceptively, that none of the women to whom I made love were what I wanted as my wife."

Nerissa did not speak and after a moment he went on:

"The difficulty is telling you what I did feel. I have become cynical and disillusioned because whenever I met someone I imagined was different I found out all too quickly she was not what I was seeking, not the image I had enshrined in my heart."

"But Delphine was . . . sure you were . . . going to ask her . . . to . . . marry you."

"What I was asking her was—something very different."

"She told me that too . . . but she was convinced you would . . . change your mind."

There was a faint twist to the Duke's lips as he said:

"Your sister is very beautiful, but I realise now that her beauty is but a pale reflection of yours."

Nerissa remembered that Harry had said the same thing and she said quickly:

"But . . . you must not . . . think like that . . . and although I . . . love you . . . I could not be happy with you if I . . . thought I had . . . hurt Delphine."

There was a little silence before the Duke said in an incredulous tone:

"Are you really saying, Nerissa, that you intend to refuse me?"

"How can I do anything else?" Nerissa asked unhappily, "I love you . . . you know I love you . . . but if I marry you . . . Delphine will curse us as you have been cursed before . . . and perhaps her curse would work . . .

and we would...lose each other...then I would... want to...die!"

"You cannot—you must not say such things!" the Duke said, pulling Nerissa against him. "Do you really believe that having found you I could lose you again?"

He looked down into her eyes as if to convince himself she was speaking sincerely. Then he said:

"You are mine! You are what I prayed I would find but feared did not exist! Then suddenly, when I walked into your father's kitchen, of all improbable places, I saw someone so perfect, so completely spiritually beautiful, that for a moment I could not believe my eyes!"

"Did you...really feel like that?" Nerissa asked.

"All that, and a great deal more," the Duke said. "Yet because I am human I tried to pretend to myself that I was merely bemused by the excellent dinner you cooked for me, and the very good wine I drank."

He was smiling as he added:

"At the same time, my precious, I was determined to see you again, which was why I invited your father to Lyn."

"Delphine did not want me to come."

"I was well aware of that," the Duke said, "but if your sister has a will of iron, so have I, and however determinedly you tried to refuse me, I would have brought you here on some pretext or other."

He searched her face before he asked:

"Do you know how precious you are? Ever since you have been here, my love has been increasing hour by hour and minute by minute."

"But you have ignored me today...you have not... talked to me," Nerissa said.

"I did not dare to do so until I had sorted things out

in my mind. Besides, I am not so stupid as not to know that had your sister realised what I was feeling she might have upset you."

Nerissa gave a little cry.

"She must . . . never know!"

"She will have to know one day," the Duke said, "for I intend that you will be my wife, Nerissa. In fact, I cannot live without you!"

"You will . . . have to!" Nerissa cried. "I love you! I love you desperately . . . but I can never . . . never marry you! How could I . . . face Delphine when she is . . . absolutely determined . . . absolutely sure you will ask her to marry you?"

The Duke put his fingers under Nerissa's chin to tilt her small face up to his.

"Look at me, my precious," he said. "Look into my eyes and tell me in your heart and soul that you really believe that feeling as we do, we can go on without each other."

Nerissa looked at him. Then the tears came into her eyes, blinding him from her sight.

"I know . . . what you are . . . saying," she said brokenly, "and I feel . . . the same. I love you until there is nothing else but . . . you in the . . . whole world. But I know that we cannot take our . . . happiness at Delphine's . . . expense. I know too that if we did so . . . I would always be afraid."

The Duke looked at her for a long moment. Then he said:

"Because we are so close to each other I understand what you are feeling, my darling. So I am going to say something, and I want you to listen very carefully."

"You know I will . . . listen to anything you . . . tell me," Nerissa said in a broken little voice.

"Then I swear before God that you will be my wife, that you will belong to me, and that we will find happiness together. That is a vow that I will not break!"

Because Nerissa knew there was nothing she could say, she gave a little sob and lay her face against his neck.

He held her very close and she knew his lips were on her hair.

For a long time they just stood there, and there was something in the closeness of him that made Nerissa feel as if she were in a stronghold of safety and love where nothing could hurt or harm her, and she would never be alone again.

It was an illusion, of course it was an illusion, yet for the moment she was his, and he hers.

The way he had spoken when he made his vow seemed to echo on the atmosphere around them.

Then the Duke took his arms from her and very gently lifted the wreath from her head.

He put it into the secret drawer and pushed it back into place.

Then he said:

"I must go back, my darling, to the Ball Room. I want you to go to sleep and not worry about anything. I love you, and you have to trust me."

"I do . . . trust you!" Nerissa said. "But promise me you will not do . . . anything that is . . . wrong."

"Because everything about you is right," the Duke said, "I would never do anything that you would feel was wrong or did not measure up to your ideals."

"How can you say anything so . . . wonderful?" Nerissa asked.

"I say it because it is true, because I love you, and because, although you may not believe it for the moment, our life together is going to be very different from any-thing either of us has ever expected."

"I . . . I must not . . . think about it," Nerissa said in a whisper.

"You must think about it," the Duke said, "and not of the obstacles which at the moment stand in our way, but which I intend to disperse, although I do not wish to discuss it now."

He looked at her for a long moment before he drew her once again into his arms and held her close against him.

"All I want you to remember, all I have to say, is that I love you," he said very quietly. "You are mine, Nerissa, and neither God nor man will ever make me give you up."

Then he was kissing her and the rapture and wonder of it carried them once again towards the stars.

chapter seven

AFTER Nerissa had gone to bed the Duke went back to the party in the Ball Room.

He then proceeded to manage with great tact to persuade the neighbours who had been invited to leave fairly early, although they were not aware that he was doing so.

When there was only the house party left, he told the Band to play "God Save the King," which meant that the party was over.

"It is too early, Talbot!" Delphine protested.

"I have many more excitements planned for you tomorrow, and as there is still another evening before you leave me, I would not wish you to be overtired."

She accepted this with a shrug of her shoulders and a pout of her lips, and linking her arms through his said beguilingly:

"All I want is to be with you, but we have not seen very much of each other."

"It is always difficult when there are so many other people in the house," the Duke replied, and disengaging himself went to say good night to his Aunt.

When everybody had gone upstairs he went outside to stand in the moonlight, looking up at the stars and thinking of Nerissa.

He knew he was the most fortunate man in the world in having found what every man seeks — a woman who loved him for himself and who knew when he kissed her had given him her heart and soul.

When he went back into the house the nightforeman had extinguished most of the candles, leaving only enough light for the Duke to see his way up the stairs towards his own room.

He walked along the corridor which led to the Master Suite and as he did so he was aware that at the other end of it there was a man approaching.

Because the Duke was thinking of Nerissa, he had no wish to have a banal conversation with anybody.

He therefore slipped into the shadows of one of the doorways wondering who his roving guest could be, and where he was going.

A moment later he realised there was no reason for him to hide, as the man, wearing a long robe which almost touched the floor, very quietly opened the door of one of the bedrooms and disappeared inside.

For a moment the Duke found it incredible and thought he must be mistaken, but as he continued towards his own bedroom he saw lying on the floor outside the door that had just been opened a pink rose.

He bent down to pick it up, and as he walked on with it in his hand he was smiling.

Nerissa felt that the day had been long-drawn-out and everything had somehow been flat.

She knew it was because the party was coming to an end and several of the guests had already left.

Although the Duke had arranged a race for the gentlemen in the morning, and a driving contest in the afternoon, for her there was something in the atmosphere which was lacking.

She knew the answer was that it was impossible for her to take part, naturally, in anything that was happening.

One moment she felt wildly elated, as she had when she went to bed the previous night, because the Duke loved her and she loved him.

Then inevitably there came a reaction and she touched the depths of despair, feeling that whatever he might say, it was impossible for her to marry him.

"I have saved him from one curse," she told herself over and over again. "How could I make him subject to another?"

Because she had always been slightly frightened of Delphine, she felt that any curse her sister put upon the Duke would somehow prove effective.

Anyway, she knew that she herself would be vividly conscious of it, and that would undoubtedly spoil their happiness.

"I love him! I love him!" she said despairingly, "but the words I said as a 'forget-me-not' will come true, and he will forget me."

It seemed to Nerissa there were only two people in the party who were supremely happy, and one of them was her father.

He was enjoying every moment of his inspection of Lyn and complaining only that it all had to be done in such a hurry. As the house had taken nearly forty years to build, he could hardly be expected to appreciate it all in the same number of hours.

If he was enthralled, Harry, with a promise of a horse from the Duke, was so exuberant that it was he alone who kept everyone laughing at luncheon and again at dinner.

It was a much smaller party in the evening and the majority of the men were close friends of the Duke who had, Nerissa thought, a really sincere wish for his happiness.

Yet Delphine, for some reason Nerissa did not understand, was piqued with him, and having at first tried pouting at him and complaining in a low voice, was by the end of the meal doing her best to make him jealous by flirting quite outrageously with Lord Locke.

The latter was only too willing to oblige, but because Nerissa was sure he really loved her sister, she thought it was cruel of Delphine to use him as a weapon against another man.

After dinner the Duke had arranged for some local performers to entertain them with mouth organs, concertinas, and bells, on which they were very skilful.

Ordinarily Nerissa would have enjoyed it enormously because it was something quite new.

But now she kept thinking that the minutes were ticking by. Tomorrow they would leave and she had no idea if the Duke had any plans for them to meet again.

She wondered to herself if in fact he had accepted what she had said to him the night before and had decided there was no point in their continuing to argue about it.

At last, although actually it was still quite early, Marcus Stanley said he was going to bed, and the Duke suggested they should all do the same.

Just for a moment, when Nerissa touched his hand to say good night, she felt the vibrations of his love surging towards her, but because she was afraid that Delphine might notice she dared not look at him.

She only lowered her head and walked slowly up the stairs behind her father.

Once again the Duke was left alone without any guests, but this time he did not go outside as he had done the previous evening.

Instead, he walked to the Duchess's Suite, and entered the small Dressing Room. Then he went to the chest and tried to open the secret drawer as Nerissa had done.

He was not as skilful as she had been, and it took him a long time before he found the place that he sought in the corner and the exact pressure he should put on it.

Then the drawer opened he and he saw the wreath inside it.

It was some time later that he walked back the way he had come, and now having stopped in his own room for a moment he went on down the wide corridor to where the previous night he had seen a pink rose lying on the floor.

Now there was no pink rose, and without knocking he opened the door and went inside.

There were only two candles lit in the very beautiful bedroom, but they afforded enough light for the Duke to see Delphine, wearing only a diaphanous négligée clasped, in the arms of Lord Locke.

He was kissing her passionately, and it was a second or two before they were aware they were not alone.

There ensued a violent exchange of words in which the Duke accused Lord Locke of behaving improperly, and Lord Locke informed the Duke he considered himself insulted.

The two men raged at each other while Delphine tried ineffectively to stop them behaving in such an inflammatory manner.

Then suddenly Lord Locke said in a voice that seemed to ring out around the room:

"I demand satisfaction, Lynchester! I will allow no man to speak to me as you have done."

"I am only too willing to meet you," the Duke replied. "It is time you were taught a lesson in behaviour."

"Then when and where?" Lord Locke asked through clenched teeth.

"I have no intention of waiting until dawn," the Duke replied. "We will fight now in the Riding School, and you may find a lead bullet in your arm will cool your ardour for the next few weeks."

"That remains to be seen," Lord Locke replied, "but I accept your suggestion."

"I will meet you in an hour's time," the Duke snapped, "and as we do not want more people than is necessary to be aware of what we are doing, I suggest we content ourselves with one Second each. I choose Charles Seeham, Wilterham can be the referee, and Lionel Hampton was a doctor before he became an explorer."

"I commend your efficiency!" Lord Locke said sarcastically.

Delphine however gave a cry of horror.

"No, no! You cannot do this! You cannot fight over me! Think of the scandal it would cause when it was known that I was involved! I will not allow you to do this!"

"It is something you cannot prevent," the Duke said,

"and because I think, Delphine, you were instrumental in inviting such a situation, I suggest you come and watch."

"I have every intention of doing so," Delphine replied. "I think you are behaving abominably—both of you! But you must both swear that whatever the outcome, neither of you will talk about it!"

"I think we both know how to behave where you are concerned," the Duke said. "At any rate, I do!"

"As you are insulting me again," Lord Locke said angrily, "I shall make double sure, Lynchester, that it is your arm which is in a sling, and I hope for months rather than weeks!"

The Duke only made an ironical bow and walked from the bedroom, saying as he did so:

"In half an hour. I will make the arrangements!"

As he left Delphine flung herself against Lord Locke.

"You must not do it! You cannot fight him, Anthony!" she cried. "You know what a good shot he is!"

"No better than I am!" Lord Locke replied. "How dare he insult me in such a manner? Or, if it comes to that, walk into your bedroom without knocking!"

"I beg you to cry off . . ." Delphine began.

But Lord Locke was disentangling himself from her clinging arms, and like the Duke he walked from the bedroom in a purposeful manner, which told her better than words that he had no intention of giving in to her pleading.

Hastily she dressed herself, and putting a fur wrap over her gown went down the stairs and left the house by a side door for the Riding School.

It was a building which had already been much admired by Marcus Stanley. It had been built first at the same time as the house, and after it was burnt down, had been reconstructed and eventually redecorated and considerably improved by Inigo Jones.

It still preserved characteristics of all these periods.

When Delphine entered the School it was to find the two contestants already there with their Seconds who were Lord John Fellowes and Sir Charles Seeham, and Lord Wilterham, who was to be the referee.

They were standing in the centre of the School, but when the Duke saw Delphine he walked towards her and taking her by the hand helped her up a small staircase which led her to the Spectators' Balcony.

"From here you can watch me teach Locke a lesson he will not forget in a hurry!" the Duke said.

"It would be far more sensible," Delphine replied coldly, "if you would both stop making fools of yourselves and endangering my reputation!"

"That is something neither of us can do," the Duke answered. "Of course I know you will wish me good luck."

"Yes—naturally," Delphine said, "but I do beg of you not to hurt Anthony."

"I hope you will say the same thing to him!" the Duke retorted sarcastically.

He kissed Delphine's hand perfunctorily, and leaving her to sit in the front of the balcony, went down the stairs to join the others.

Lord Wilterham, as the referee, took over.

"Now you both know the rules," he said. "I will count aloud up to ten, during which time you will walk away from each other for ten paces. Then you will turn and fire."

There was no need for the Duke and Lord Locke to answer him.

They both, as Lord Wilterham knew, had taken part in several duels at one time or another, and the Duke had never been the loser.

The two Seconds went to their appointed places at each end of the School.

Then as Lord Wilterham began counting, the Duke and Lord Locke, who had been standing back to back, started to walk away from each other.

It seemed as if the referee was taking a long time.

". . . Seven . . . eight . . . nine . . . ten—fire!"

The two men turned, two shots rang out, echoing and seeming to reecho around the high-roofed building.

Then slowly, so slowly that it was hard to believe it was happening, Lord Locke fell to the ground.

The Duke stood still staring at his opponent incredulously, then suddenly John Fellowes, Lord Locke's Second, came running towards him.

"You hit him in the heart, Talbot!"

"It is impossible!" the Duke exclaimed.

"No, it is the truth. He must have faced you when he fired, but there is no mistake and I am sure he is dead!"

The Duke was frozen in his astonishment.

At the same time his own Second, Charles Seeham, who had also been bending over Lord Locke at the other end of the School, came up to him.

"You have killed him, Talbot!" he said. "He is still alive, but Hampton says it is not a question of hours but minutes! You will have to get out of the country as quickly as you can! Otherwise you will be arrested and have to stand trial."

The Duke's lips tightened, but he did not speak, and Charles Seeham went on:

"It is the only thing you can do. You cannot risk being

arrested when Delphine Bramwell's name will come into it!"

As he spoke Delphine, who had come down from the balcony, came towards them.

"What is happening?" she asked. "Is Anthony hurt?"

"I am afraid he is dying," Charles Seeham said sympathetically.

"Oh, God, no! I do not believe it! How can you say such a thing! I must go and look for myself!"

She would have run to the other end of the School had not Charles Seeham held on to her wrist.

"Do not look at him, Delphine," he said gently. "It is not something a woman should see. He has been shot in the heart!"

"How could you do this?" Delphine asked of the Duke in a low voice.

"You must know I did not mean this to happen," he replied.

"We all know that," Charles Seeham agreed, "but it has! You must get away, Talbot. Think of the family, think of Delphine, and leave. For God's sake, leave!"

"I suppose it is the only thing I can do," the Duke said dully.

He reached towards Delphine and took her hand in his.

He drew her towards the farther entrance of the Riding School as the other men ran back to where Lord Locke lay on the ground being treated by the doctor.

As they reached the doorway the Duke said:

"You will understand, Delphine, that for your sake as well as my own, I have to go into exile. In that way there will be very little scandal and by the time I am able to return, what has happened will be forgotten."

144

Delphine was very pale, and as the Duke was speaking she kept glancing over her shoulder towards the other end of the Riding School.

"There is one thing I want to ask you, Delphine," the Duke said quietly. "Will you come with me?"

"With . . . you?" she repeated rather stupidly.

"I am asking you to marry me," he said. "We shall have to live abroad for three years, perhaps longer, but I am sure we can find ways of passing the time enjoyably."

"Three years?" Delphine exclaimed in horror. "It will be as long as that?"

"Three to six," the Duke said, "is the usual time in such circumstances, and I cannot hope it will be less than three."

Delphine stared at him, her eyes dark and frightened in her lovely face.

Then when she would have spoken Charles Seeham came back.

"Wilterham has told me to warn you not to waste any more time," he said to the Duke. "In his position he says he will have to report what has happened in the morning, and by that time you must be across the Channel."

"Is there no chance of Locke living?" the Duke asked slowly.

"A chance in a million," Charles Seeham replied, "and I would not bet on that!"

"Tell Wilterham I am leaving immediately," the Duke said.

Charles Seeham did not say any more, but hurried away and the Duke said:

"Is it yes or no, Delphine?"

She gave a little sigh.

"I am sorry, Talbot. You know I wanted to marry you, but not like this—not in exile—away from everything I care about."

"I understand," the Duke said, "and I am sorry, Delphine. Once I have gone, you must deny any knowledge of what has happened or that you were in any way involved."

"I shall be very careful to do that," she said in a hard voice, and the Duke left her.

Once he was in the house he walked quickly up the stairs, along the corridor to where Nerissa's bedroom was, next to her father's.

He opened the door quietly and saw by the light of one candle that Nerissa was kneeling by her bed in prayer.

For a moment, concentrating on her prayers, she did not hear him.

Then, as if it were his presence rather than any noise he might have made that alerted her, she turned her head.

Surprised, and at the same time unable to prevent an irresistible gladness illuminating her face, she rose slowly to her feet as the Duke shut the door behind him, and moving towards her took her hand in his.

"Listen, my darling," he said. "I have been involved in a duel with Anthony Locke, and quite by accident—I promise you it was not intentional—I have wounded him mortally!"

Nerissa gave a little cry of horror.

"Mortally?"

"He is still alive, but Hampton thinks it is a question of an hour at the outside before he dies!"

"Oh . . . how . . . terrible!" Nerissa murmured.

"You will understand that in the circumstances, in order to avoid the scandal that will ensue if I am arrested,

146

I have to go into exile, and I am asking you to come with me."

For a moment Nerissa's eyes lit up. Then she said almost beneath her breath:

"B-but . . . Delphine!"

"Because the duel was over Delphine," the Duke said, "I asked her if she would come with me as my wife. She refused!"

Nerissa drew in her breath.

"She . . . really . . . refused?"

"She said she could not face exile for three years away from everything that she cares for."

The light was back in Nerissa's eyes as if a thousand candles burned within them.

"Then I may come with you?" she asked almost inaudibly.

"I am begging you on my knees to do so."

"Oh . . . Talbot!"

The words were a cry of happiness.

He did not kiss her. He only said:

"There is no time to be lost. We leave as quickly as possible! Dress yourself and I will send somebody to collect your luggage."

He looked down into her eyes for a second. Then he was gone and Nerissa was alone.

For a moment she could hardly believe it was happening. Then she knew that they were both free to tell each other of their love, and nothing mattered except that they could be together.

Hastily she began to dress, aware as she did so that because she had told Mary she was leaving early in the morning her trunk was already packed, except for the gown she had worn for dinner.

Hanging in the wardrobe for her journey home was only the pretty cape and muslin gown she had worn on her arrival at Lyn.

She was just tying the ribbons of her bonnet when there was a knock on the door and the Duke's valet, Banks, came in followed by a young footman.

"Is your trunk ready, Miss?" he asked.

"You have only to strap it up," Nerissa replied.

"His Grace's downstairs, Miss, waiting for you."

He and the footman carried the trunk out of the room and down the corridor.

Nerissa looked around quickly to see that she had not forgotten anything, then feeling as if she had wings on her feet she ran down the stairs to where the Duke was waiting for her.

He too had changed, and through the front door Nerissa could see his travelling carriage, drawn by six horses and beside it two outriders.

There was no one to see them off and the Duke, taking Nerissa by the hand, drew her down the steps and into the carriage.

As they drove away she could hardly believe it was happening, that she had not stepped into some strange dream which might turn into a nightmare.

Then she was aware of the pressure of the Duke's fingers on hers, the closeness of him beside her, and the fact that they were alone together.

Only as they turned out of the great iron gates did she cry almost incoherently:

"I . . . I should have left a . . . note for Papa . . . to tell him what . . . has happened."

"I have thought of that," the Duke said. "I have not only left *him* a letter but also one for Harry."

"You think of . . . everything!"

"I think of you," the Duke answered, "and how much I love you."

He put his arm around her as he spoke and drew her against him.

For a moment neither of them spoke, then with his other hand he undid the ribbons of her bonnet and threw it onto the seat opposite.

As she put her head on his shoulder he said:

"You are certain, my precious, that you will not regret coming away with me in such haste? You realise if Locke dies you will be exiled from England for what may seem a very long time."

"It does not matter where we are . . . as long as I can be with you," Nerissa said, "but I shall be . . . worrying in case you find it . . . boring to be . . . alone with only . . . me."

The Duke did not answer, he merely kissed her and there was no further need for words.

* * *

They reached Dover when the sun was rising over the horizon.

It was in fact only a little more than twenty miles from Lyn, and the Duke's superb horses reached it in record time.

Nerissa expected they would drive straight to the harbour, where the Duke had told her his yacht was waiting.

"Will the Captain be expecting you?" she asked.

"I did in fact send a groom ahead," the Duke replied, "but in any case, the standing orders are that my yacht is always ready to sail at any time. So once we are aboard, there will be no delay in leaving these shores for France, where we will be safe."

"That is . . . all that . . . matters," Nerissa said in a low voice.

"There is something we have to do first," the Duke said.

Before she could ask him what it was, the horses came to a standstill and she saw through the window they were outside a small Chapel which stood at the end of the harbour.

She looked at the Duke in surprise and he explained:

"This is where the fishermen pray before they go to sea and where their wives pray they will return safely. I think, my darling, you will find in it the right atmosphere for us to become man and wife."

For a moment Nerissa looked at him incredulously.

Then to her surprise he opened a leather case which she had noticed during the journey was lying on the seat opposite them.

He took from it the wreath of diamonds and pearls she had found in the secret drawer in the Duchess's Room, and with it an exquisitely delicate lace veil.

Very gently the Duke put the veil over Nerissa's fair hair and placed the wreath on top.

Then as the coachman opened the door they stepped out and walked up the few steps which led to the Chapel.

As they reached the open door Nerissa could hear an organ playing softly.

Inside, the Chapel was in darkness, save for the light of six candles on the altar, in front of which stood a Clergyman wearing a white surplice.

Nerissa looked up and saw that draped from the rounded ceiling there hung fishermen's nets, and she thought they gave the place an air of mystery.

At the same time she was conscious, as the Duke had

said, that the Chapel had an atmosphere of sanctity and of devotion which made it vibrate for her with the faith that she had always had herself.

The Duke lifted her travelling cape from her shoulders and laid it on an adjacent pew.

Then as they walked up the aisle she knew that in her white dress with the lace veil flowing from her head to the ground and the diamonds sparkling above it she was the bride he had always wanted.

She felt that while the Chapel appeared to be empty, it was in spirit filled with those who loved them and would not wish them to marry without their blessing.

Nerissa was certain that her own mother was there as well as the Duke's.

The unhappy Duchess was there too, just as she had seen her in her dream, only now because the hidden wreath had been found and the curse lifted she looked happy and at peace.

Now she could leave this earth and be with the husband she loved, and who had loved her.

It was strange, Nerissa thought, how she was so certain of this. And yet she knew it was true and that the Duke would believe it too when she told him about it.

Then as the Priest married them she knew that they had been blessed, as few married couples were privileged to be, by a love that had endured many sacrifices and would continue for eternity.

The strains of the organ accompanied them back down the aisle, and as they reached the door of the Chapel the sunshine dazzled Nerissa's eyes and she knew it prefigured the happiness they would find together.

It took only a few minutes for their carriage to reach the Duke's yacht, which was called *The Sea Horse*, and which was much larger than she expected.

Then, as the Duke told her, as soon as they were aboard, the yacht moved slowly out of harbour on the morning tide.

He would not allow her to watch the coast of England disappear behind them as they sailed for the coast of France.

Instead, he took her below into the most comfortable and attractive cabin she could imagine and told her she was to go to sleep.

"You have been through a great deal," he said quietly, "and we have our whole future in front of us, so now I want you to sleep. We will talk everything over later when you wake."

She wanted to protest. At the same time she was indeed very tired.

It had all been so dramatic, so unexpected, and she had in fact slept very little the night before because she had been so thrilled and aroused by the Duke's kisses.

Now he did not kiss her passionately but gently and tenderly, as if she were infinitely precious.

Then almost before she realised what was happening, she found herself alone in the cabin.

Because she wanted to please him, she did as he told her and got into bed.

* * *

"Do you realise," Nerissa asked her husband, "we have been married exactly a week today!"

"I thought it was much longer!" the Duke replied.

Then as Nerissa gave an exclamation she realised he was teasing her.

"What do you feel about that week?" he asked.

They were lying side by side in the large bed that seemed almost to fill the cabin.

Nerissa turned to move closer to him, and his arm went around her, holding her tightly so that it was hard to breathe.

"You must be tired of hearing me say it," she said, "but . . . I love you!"

"Tell me about your love," the Duke commanded.

Nerissa gave a little sigh.

"Every night, after we have spent the day together, I have felt it would be impossible for me to love you more, and yet every morning when I awake I know that you have made my love for you more intense and more wonderful than it was the previous day."

"Is that really true?" the Duke asked.

As he spoke he swept her fair hair back from her forehead to look down at her.

Because he was so happy Nerissa knew that he looked younger and even more handsome than he had ever before.

There was no longer that sarcastic twist to his lips or the cynical note in his voice.

Everything he said or did seemed to vibrate with the love which, as she had said, increased every moment that they were together, until she felt it impossible that any two people could be so ecstatically happy.

"It is fun to stop at these little French harbours," Nerissa went on as if she were thinking it out for herself, "and go ashore to eat such delicious food. The only trouble is that when I am with you it is difficult to concentrate on what I am eating, but only of how exciting your kisses are!"

"I am glad you are not bored with them," the Duke said, "because I have a great many more to give you."

He turned her face up to his as he spoke and kissed her at first gently, then as he felt her body quiver against him, more passionately.

"Could anything be more exciting?" he asked. "I thought, my darling, you were beautiful when I first saw you, but you are infinitely more lovely now. I think it is because you are now a woman and no longer a young girl."

What he said made Nerissa blush, and he said:

"It may make you shy, but I think, my precious, when I teach you about love I make you feel like a woman."

"You teach me so many things," Nerissa replied, "and I want to learn more and more and especially how to make you . . . love me."

"Do you doubt that is what I do already?"

"I hope so," Nerissa said, "but, darling, I have to make up for so many things in your life, and most of all for Lyn!"

She spoke with a tremble in her voice because she was always afraid the Duke was yearning for Lyn, and feeling that however exciting the things they did together, it was not the same as being in the home he loved and to which he belonged.

"I am sure everything at Lyn is all right," the Duke said in a different tone. "I told your brother to keep my horses exercised, which I am sure he is only too willing to do, and not to leave until your father has all the information necessary for his book."

Nerissa gave a little cry.

"Did you really say that? How could you be so kind and so thoughtful?"

"I also told my Steward," the Duke went on, "that when they did decide to leave he was to send two servants with them to look after them at Queen's Rest."

Nerissa gave a little choke as she hid her face against his neck and said:

"You are making me feel ashamed that I have not worried more about Papa. You may think I am making excuses, but I find it so difficult to think of . . . anything or . . . anybody but . . . you!"

"That is exactly why, quite selfishly, I thought of your father and Harry for you. If you are to worry about anybody, you are to worry about me, and that is an order!"

"I . . . worry about your . . . happiness."

"Quite right," the Duke approved. "I want you to concentrate on me, and I shall be very jealous if you think of anybody else."

"It would be very . . . difficult for me to . . . do so," Nerissa admitted.

Then in a very small voice, cuddling close against him, she said:

"It may seem . . . strange . . . but I have never asked you about the duel . . . and why it took place."

"I do not want to talk about it," the Duke said. "But as I am sure you are curious as to what is happening at Lyn, as I admit I am, we are now on our way to Calais, where I have arranged for my secretary to meet me. He will have crossed the Channel early this morning, bringing me the very latest news."

Nerissa was still for a moment. Then suddenly she was frightened.

"You . . . do not think there will be . . . people waiting to . . . arrest you and take you back to . . . England?"

"They cannot do that when I am on foreign soil," the Duke replied. "No order from a British Magistrate has any power across the Channel. So do not worry, my precious. Leave me to do the worrying. But I felt that like me you would be curious and wish to know what is happening in our absence."

Nerissa did not like to confess that because she had been so ecstatically happy with the Duke she had hardly given a thought to the chaos they had left behind at Lyn.

It must have been a shock to the whole household to find in the morning that the Duke had disappeared, and now that she thought about it she was afraid that though Delphine had refused to accompany him, she might have been extremely angry that she had taken her place.

She however did not wish to worry the Duke with this thought, and she managed to say very little until when just before noon the yacht moved smoothly into the harbour at Calais.

The Duke went ashore alone as Nerissa had expected he would do.

She felt sure he would want to safeguard her from any shocks that might be awaiting them and would prefer to tell her about it when he returned to the ship.

At the same time she could not help feeling agitated, and going up on deck, she stared at the Quay though she knew she could not yet expect to see any sign of the Duke.

With a great effort she forced herself to go and sit on the other side of the yacht and look out to sea.

It was nearly luncheontime before the Duke returned, and when he came aboard Nerissa ran to him with a little cry.

She knew before he spoke that he was feeling happy and all was well.

"It is . . . good news?"

"Very good."

They sat down on the wooden seat, and taking her hand in his, the Duke said:

"My darling, by a miracle Anthony Locke has recovered from his injuries and is alive!"

Nerissa gave a little gasp.

"Alive?" she managed to whisper.

"Alive!" the Duke repeated. "This means that when we are ready to do so, which will be after we have finished our honeymoon, we can go home."

Nerissa stared at him incredulously.

Then suddenly the tears were running down her cheeks and she hid her face against him.

"You are not crying, my precious?" the Duke asked.

"They are tears . . . of . . . h-happiness," Nerissa said. "I have been . . . praying . . . praying desperately . . . that things might not . . . be as bad as they s-seemed . . . and you would not be . . . exiled for l-long."

"Your prayers have been answered," the Duke said, "and I cannot allow you to cry. I want you laughing and happy as I intend you to be for the rest of our lives together."

He kissed her until she was smiling, and when she went below to get ready for luncheon he walked to the bow of the yacht to look at the Channel which lay between France and England.

He thought that in three weeks, perhaps a month, he would take Nerissa home.

She would never know, he thought, how carefully he and Anthony Locke had plotted the whole episode between them. They had each sworn to the other that no one except the friends who had played their supporting parts in the duel should ever know the truth.

Lord Locke had told the Duke when he challenged him that he was genuinely in love with Delphine and she was in love with him, but the difficulty was that he had nothing to offer her, not even a house.

The Duke then said it had been in his mind for some time that Anthony Locke, who was an extremely experienced horseman, might, if it pleased him, take over the management of his racehorses.

"There is an excellent house at Newmarket to go with the job," he told him, "and if I make your salary high enough to include a house in London, I think Delphine will have everything she desires."

Lord Locke had been certain that although Delphine had been spoilt by the adulation she received, he could in such circumstances make her happy, and he had therefore agreed to everything the Duke suggested.

This included a duel with blank cartridges, and a way for the Duke to go into exile while Lord Locke pretened to be at death's door.

Every detail had been planned so that no one would ever suspect that what happened had been contrived, including Lionel Hampton's faking a most realistic scar on Lord Locke's heart.

The Duke's secretary was now able to inform that His Lordship was in far better health than might have been expected in the circumstances, and he and Lady Bramwell were planning to be married in two weeks time.

The Duke had sent them his congratulations and he knew when he told Nerissa that her sister was to be happily married the last cloud would be removed from her sunlit sky.

"I have been clever!" he told himself complacently. "At the same time I genuinely believe that it was Nerissa's finding of the unhappy Duchess's wreath that lifted the curse that has always menaced the Dukes of Lynchester."

It was a fascinating story, he thought, that could never be written because the charade of the duel and his and Lord Locke's enacting of it must always remain untold.

At the same time, he was deeply grateful that everything had gone so smoothly and he knew that Nerissa, with her sweetness, her purity, and her sensitivity would bring a new era of happiness to Lyn.

He hoped never again would he undergo the suspense of a desperate gambler, staking everything he possessed on the turn of a card, when he asked Delphine to marry him.

By the mercy of Heaven she had refused and the game was his!

It was not until later that night, after they had kissed each other under the stars and then gone below because they both wanted to be closer still, that the Duke holding Nerissa in his arms, said:

"I have something to tell you, my darling, which I think will please you."

"What is it?" she asked. "I have felt all day you have been hiding something from me."

"You are not to read my thoughts," he said. "You are far too perceptive about me! I am beginning to believe that you are a witch!"

"If I am perceptive," Nerissa replied, "it is only because I love you, and my love makes me listen to every intonation of your voice and makes me see every expression in your eyes."

"I would feel nervous if I did not feel the same about you."

He kissed her forehead before he said:

"Are you listening to what I have to tell you?"

"Of course I am," Nerissa replied. "Is it something happy?"

"I know you will think so. Your sister, Delphine, is to marry Anthony Locke!"

Nerissa gave a little cry that seemed to ring out in the cabin.

"That is what I wanted," she said. "I knew that she loved him as he loves her . . . but she longed even more to be a Duchess."

"I am sure now she has found that love means far more than a strawberry-leaf contest," the Duke said.

"I am glad . . . so very, very glad," Nerissa said, "and now I shall not be afraid of meeting her when we go home."

"I will not have you afraid of anybody or anything," the Duke said. "All those fears and worries are over and all you have to do, my beloved, is to extend the love that you have given to me to everybody at Lyn and all those who come to us there."

"We will make it a house of love," Nerissa murmured, "but we can do that only if we go on loving each other . . . as we do now."

"And which I have every intention of doing."

The Duke raised himself on his elbow to look down at her in the light from the candle lantern he had burning beside the bed.

"I was thinking today," he said seriously, "that I was the most fortunate man in the whole world to have found you. Just suppose your sister had not wished to show me her ancient Elizabethan home and her distinguished father? I might never have met you!"

Nerissa gave a little cry of horror.

"Oh, my darling, I might have gone all through my

160

life without knowing you even existed, except that Harry would have talked about you, and told me, as he said he ought not to do, that you were a 'devil with the women'!"

The Duke laughed.

"That may have been true in the past, but now as far as women are concerned I am a Saint, and no one could tempt me, however much they tried."

"You are . . . quite sure of that?" Nerissa asked.

"Quite sure! I can be tempted by only one woman when I find her so enthralling, so exciting, so completely and utterly satisfying, that as far as I am concerned there is no other woman in the whole world!"

Nerissa gave a little cry of delight.

"Oh, darling, that is what I wanted you to say! I could not bear to be made jealous of all those lovely ladies who fawned on you and made me feel very insignificant and just a little forget-me-not."

The Duke's lips were very close to hers, and his hands were touching her body as he asked:

"Do you really think I could forget you? Do you really think that anybody else could make me feel as I do now?"

"How . . . do you feel?" Nerissa asked.

"Very much in love, very excited, and irresistibly tempted by the most beautiful woman I have ever seen."

He did not wait for her to say anything, but his lips came down on hers and as the fire leapt within him and he felt the flames flicker within Nerissa, he knew they were complete in one person.

This was a spiritual ecstasy that was different from anything he had ever known before, and it carried them into the sky, where there was only love, and more love.

The love that lasts for eternity and beyond.

ABOUT THE AUTHOR

Barbara Cartland, the world's most famous romantic novelist, who is also an historian, playwright, lecturer, political speaker and television personality, has now written over 400 books and sold over 390 million books the world over.

She has also had many historical works published and has written four autobiographies as well as the biographies of her mother and that of her brother, Ronald Cartland, who was the first Member of Parliament to be killed in the last war. This book has a preface by Sir Winston Churchill and has just been republished with an introduction by Sir Arthur Bryant.

Love at the Helm, a novel written with the help and inspiration of the late Admiral of the Fleet, the Earl Mountbatten of Burma, is being sold for the Mountbatten Memorial Trust.

Miss Cartland in 1978 sang an Album of Love Songs with the Royal Philharmonic Orchestra.

In 1976 by writing twenty-one books, she broke the world record and has continued for the following seven years with twenty-four, twenty, twenty-three, twenty-four, twenty-four, twenty-five, and twenty-three. She is in the *Guinness Book of Records* as the best-selling author in the world.

She is unique in that she was one and two in the Dalton List of Best Sellers, and one week had four books in the top twenty.

In private life Barbara Cartland, who is a Dame of the Order of St. John of Jerusalem, Chairman of the St. John Council in Hertfordshire and Deputy President of the St. John Ambulance Brigade, has also fought for better conditions and salaries for Midwives and Nurses.

Barbara Cartland is deeply interested in Vitamin Therapy and is President of the British National Association for health. Her book *The Magic of Honey* has sold throughout the world and is translated into many languages. Her designs "Decorating with Love" are being sold all over the U.S.A., and the National Home Fashions league named her in 1981, "Woman of Achievement."

In 1984 she received at Kennedy Airport America's Bishop Wright Air Industry Award for her contribution to the development of aviation; in 1931 she and two R.A.F. Officers thought of, and carried, the first aeroplane-towed glider air-mail.

Barbara Cartland's Romances (a book of cartoons) has been published in Great Britain and the U.S.A., as well as a cookery book, *The Romance of Food*, and *Getting Older, Growing Younger*. She has recently written a children's pop-up picture book, entitled *Princess to the Rescue*.

More romance from
BARBARA CARTLAND

Prices may be slightly higher in Canada.

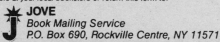

BARBARA CARTLAND

Called after her own
beloved Camfield Place,
each Camfield novel of love
by Barbara Cartland
is a thrilling, never-before published
love story by the greatest romance
writer of all time.